The Love Letters of Mary Wollstonecraft to Gilbert Imlay by Mary Wollstonecraft

lited by William Godwin

Mary Wollstonecraft was born on 27th April 1759 in Spitalfields, London. Although her family had a comfortable income much was squandered by her father leading the family to become financially diminished. Wollstonecraft struck out on her own in 1778 and accepted a job as a lady's companion. Frustrated by the limited career options open to respectable yet poor women, she nonetheless decided to embark upon a career as an author. At the time, few women could support themselves by writing.

She learned French and German and translated texts. She also wrote reviews, primarily of novels, for Johnson's periodical, the Analytical Review.

Wollstonecraft also pursued a relationship with the artist Henry Fuseli. Boldly she proposed a platonic living arrangement with Fuseli and his wife. Fuseli's wife was shocked and the relationship was severed.

In December 1792 she left for France to view first hand the revolutionary events that she had just celebrated in her recent 'Vindication of the Rights of Men' (1790) and that had brought her immediate fame.

France declared war on Britain in February 1793 and Wollstonecraft tried to leave for Switzerland but was denied permission. Despite her sympathy for the revolution, life for Wollstonecraft was very uncomfortable.

Having just written the 'Rights of Woman', Wollstonecraft determined to put her ideas to the test. She alighted on and fell passionately in love with Gilbert Imlay, an American diplomat and adventurer. By now she was disillusioned by the Revolution's path. She thought the republic behaved slavishly to those in power while the government was 'venal' and 'brutal'. To protect Wollstonecraft from the prospect of arrest, Imlay made a false statement to the U.S. embassy in Paris that he had married her, automatically making her an American citizen. Wollstonecraft, now pregnant by Imlay, gave birth to her first child, Fanny, on 14th May 1794. She was overjoyed.

The winter of 1794–95 was the coldest winter in over a century. Wollstonecraft and Fanny were reduced to desperate circumstances. Wollstonecraft now had to risk leaving France and did so on 7th April 1795. She sought Imlay out but he was impassive to her pleas. In May 1795 she attempted to commit suicide, but it is thought Imlay saved her life. But it was now certain that her relationship with Imlay was over. She attempted suicide for a second time but a passing stranger witnessed her jump into the Thames and rescued her.

Gradually, Wollstonecraft returned to literary life, and to a relationship with William Godwin. Once Wollstonecraft became pregnant by him, they decided to marry so that the child would be legitimate.

On 30th August 1797, Wollstonecraft gave birth to her second daughter, Mary. During the delivery the placenta broke apart and became infected. After several days of agony, Mary Wollstonecraft died of septicemia on 10th September 1797.

Index of Contents

PREFACE

I

Of Mary Wollstonecraft's ancestors little is known, except that they were of Irish descent. Her father, Edward John Wollstonecraft, was the son of a prosperous Spitalfields manufacturer of Irish birth, from whom he inherited the sum of ten thousand pounds. He married towards the middle of the eighteenth century Elizabeth Dixon, the daughter of a gentleman in good position, of Ballyshannon, by whom he had six children: Edward, Mary, Everina, Eliza, James, and Charles. Mary, the eldest daughter and second child, was born on April 27, 1759, the birth year of Burns and Schiller, and the last year of George II.'s reign. She passed her childhood, until she was five years old, in the neighbourhood of Epping Forest, but it is doubtful whether she was born there or at Hoxton. Mr. Wollstonecraft followed no profession in particular, although from time to time he dabbled in a variety of pursuits when seized with a desire to make money. He is described as of idle, dissipated habits, and possessed of an ungovernable temper and a restless spirit that urged him to perpetual changes of residence. From Hoxton, where he squandered most of his fortune, he wandered to Essex, and then, among other places, in 1768 to Beverley, in Yorkshire. Later he took up farming at Laugharne in Pembrokeshire, but he at length grew tired of this experiment and returned once more to London. As his fortunes declined, his brutality and selfishness increased, and Mary was frequently compelled to defend her mother from his acts of personal violence, sometimes by thrusting herself bodily between him and his victim. Mrs. Wollstonecraft herself was far from being an amiable woman; a petty tyrant and a stern but incompetent ruler of her household, she treated Mary as the scapegoat of the family. Mary's early years therefore were far from being happy; what little schooling she had was spasmodic, owing to her father's migratory habits.

In her sixteenth year, when the Wollstonecrafts were once more in London, Mary formed a friendship with Fanny Blood, a young girl about her own age, which was destined to be one of the happiest events of her life. There was a strong bond of sympathy between the two friends, for Fanny contrived by her work as an artist to be the chief support of her family, as her father, like Mr. Wollstonecraft, was a lazy, drunken fellow.

Mary's new friend was an intellectual and cultured girl. She loved music, sang agreeably, was well-read too, for her age, and wrote interesting letters. It was by comparing Fanny Blood's letters with her own, that Mary first recognised how defective her education had been. She applied herself therefore to the task of increasing her slender stock of knowledge—hoping ultimately to become a governess. At length, at the age of nineteen, Mary went to Bath as companion to a tiresome and exacting old lady, a Mrs. Dawson, the widow of a wealthy London tradesman. In spite of many difficulties, she managed to retain her situation for some two years, leaving it only to attend the deathbed of her mother.

Mrs. Wollstonecraft's death (in 1780) was followed by the break-up of the home. Mary went to live temporarily with the Bloods at Walham Green, and assisted Mrs. Blood, who took in needle-work; Everina became for a short time housekeeper to her brother Edward, a solicitor; and Eliza married a Mr. Bishop.

Mr. Kegan Paul has pointed out that "all the Wollstonecraft sisters were enthusiastic, excitable, and hasty tempered, apt to exaggerate trifles, sensitive to magnify inattention into slights, and slights into studied insults. All had bad health of a kind which is especially trying to the nerves, and Eliza had in excess the family temperament and constitution." Mrs. Bishop's married life from the first was one of utter misery; they were an ill-matched pair, and her peculiar temperament evidently exasperated her husband's worst nature. His outbursts of fury and the scenes of violence of daily occurrence, for which he was responsible, were afterwards described with realistic fidelity by Mary in her novel, "The Wrongs of Women." It was plainly impossible for Mrs. Bishop to continue to live with such a man, and when, in 1782, she became dangerously ill, Mary, with her characteristic good nature, went to nurse her, and soon after assisted her in her flight from her husband.

In the following year (1783) Mary set up a school at Islington with Fanny Blood, and she was thus in a position to offer a home to her sisters, Mrs. Bishop and Everina. The school was afterwards moved to Newington Green, where Mary soon had an establishment with some twenty day scholars. After a time, emboldened by her success, she took a larger house; but unfortunately the number of her pupils did not increase in proportion to her obligations, which were now heavier than she could well meet.

From an engraving, after the painting by John Opie, R.A.

While Mary was living at Newington Green, she was introduced to Dr. Johnson, who, Godwin says, treated her with particular kindness and attention, and with whom she had a long conversation. He desired her to repeat her visit, but she was prevented from seeing him again by his last illness and death.

In the meantime Fanny Blood had impaired her health by overwork, and signs of consumption were already evident. A Mr. Hugh Skeys, who was engaged in business at Lisbon, though somewhat of a weak lover, had long admired Fanny, and wanted to marry her. It was thought that the climate of Portugal might help to restore her health, and she consented, perhaps more on that account than on any other, to become his wife. She left England in February 1785, but her health continued to grow worse. Mary's anxiety for her friend's welfare was such that, on hearing of her grave condition, she at once went off to Lisbon, and arrived after a stormy passage, only in time to comfort Fanny in her dying moments. Mary was almost broken-hearted at the loss of her friend, and she made her stay in Lisbon as short as possible, remaining only as long as was necessary for Mrs. Skeys's funeral.

She returned to England to find that the school had greatly suffered by neglect during her absence. In a letter to Mrs. Skeys's brother, George Blood, she says: "The loss of Fanny was sufficient to have thrown a cloud over my brightest days: what effect then must it have, when I am bereft of every other comfort? I have too many debts, the rent is so enormous, and where to go, without money or friends, who can point out?"

She thus realised that to continue her school was useless. But her experience as a schoolmistress was to bear fruit in the future. She had observed some of the defects of the educational methods of her time, and her earliest published effort was a pamphlet entitled, "Thoughts on the Education of Daughters," (1787). For this essay she received ten guineas, a sum that she gave to the parents of her friend, Mr. and Mrs. Blood, who were desirous of going over to Ireland.

She soon went to Ireland herself, for in the October of 1787 she became governess to the daughters of Lord Kingsborough at Michaelstown, with a salary of forty pounds a year. Lady Kingsborough in Mary's opinion was "a shrewd clever woman, a great talker.... She rouges, and in short is a fine lady without fancy or sensibility. I am almost tormented to death by dogs...." Lady Kingsborough was rather selfish and uncultured, and her chief object was the pursuit of pleasure. She pampered her dogs, much to the disgust of Mary Wollstonecraft, and neglected her children. What views she had on education were narrow. She had been accustomed to submission from her governess, but she learnt before long that Mary was not of a tractable disposition. The children, at first unruly and defiant, "literally speaking, wild Irish, unformed and not very pleasing," soon gave Mary their confidence, and before long their affection. One of her pupils, Margaret King, afterwards Lady Mountcashel, always retained the warmest regard for Mary Wollstonecraft. Lady Mountcashel continued her acquaintance with William Godwin after Mary's death, and later came across Shelley and his wife in Italy. Mary won from the children the affection that they withheld from their mother, consequently, in the autumn of 1788, when she had been with Lady Kingsborough for about a year, she received her dismissal. She had completed by this time the novel to which she gave the name of "Mary," which is a tribute to the memory of her friend Fanny Blood.

II

And now, in her thirtieth year, Mary Wollstonecraft had concluded her career as a governess, and was resolved henceforth to devote herself to literature. Her chances of success were slender indeed, for she had written nothing to encourage her for such a venture. It was her fortune, however, to make the acquaintance of Joseph Johnson, the humanitarian publisher and bookseller of St. Paul's Churchyard, who issued the works of Priestley, Horne Tooke, Gilbert Wakefield, and other men of advanced thought, and she met at his table many of the authors for whom he published, and such eminent men of the day as William Blake, Fuseli, and Tom Paine. Mr. Johnson, who afterwards proved one of her best friends, encouraged her in her literary plans. He was the publisher of her "Thoughts on the Education of Daughters," and had recognised in that little book so much promise, that when she sought his advice, he at once offered to assist her with employment.

Mary therefore settled at Michaelmas 1788 in a house in George Street, Blackfriars. She had brought to London the manuscript of her novel "Mary," and she set to work on a book for children entitled "Original Stories from Real Life." Both of these books appeared before the year was out, the latter with quaint plates by William Blake. Mary also occupied some of her time with translations from the French,

German, and even Dutch, one of which was an abridged edition of Saltzmann's "Elements of Morality," for which Blake also supplied the illustrations. Besides this work, Johnson engaged Mary as his literary adviser or "reader," and secured her services in connexion with The Analytical Review, a periodical that he had recently founded.

While she was at George Street she also wrote her "Vindication of the Rights of Man" in a letter to Edmund Burke. Her chief satisfaction in keeping up this house was to have a home where her brothers and sisters could always come when out of employment. She was never weary of assisting them either with money, or by exerting her influence to find them situations. One of her first acts when she settled in London was to send Everina Wollstonecraft to Paris to improve her French accent. Mr. Johnson, who wrote a short account of Mary's life in London at this time, says she often spent her afternoons and evenings at his house, and used to seek his advice, or unburden her troubles to him. Among the many duties she imposed on herself was the charge of her father's affairs, which must indeed have been a profitless undertaking.

The most important of Mary Wollstonecraft's labours while she was living at Blackfriars was the writing of the book that is chiefly associated with her name, "A Vindication of the Rights of Woman." This volume—now much better known by its title than its contents—was dedicated to the astute M. Talleyrand de Périgord, late Bishop of Autun, apparently on account of his authorship of a pamphlet on National Education. It is unnecessary to attempt an analysis of this strikingly original but most unequal book—modern reprints of the work have appeared under the editorship both of Mrs. Fawcett and Mrs. Pennell. It is sufficient to say that it is really a plea for a more enlightened system of education, affecting not only her own sex, but also humanity in its widest sense. Many of her suggestions have long since been put to practical use, such as that of a system of free national education, with equal advantages for boys and girls. The book contains too much theory and is therefore to a great extent obsolete. Mary Wollstonecraft protests against the custom that recognises woman as the plaything of man; she pleads rather for a friendly footing of equality between the sexes, besides claiming a new order of things for women, in terms which are unusually frank. Such a book could not fail to create a sensation, and it speedily made her notorious, not only in this country, but on the Continent, where it was translated into French. It was of course the outcome of the French Revolution; the whole work is permeated with the ideas and ideals of that movement, but whereas the French patriots demanded rights for men, she made the same demands also for women.

It is evident that the great historical drama then being enacted in France had made a deep impression on Mary's mind—its influence is stamped on every page of her book, and it was her desire to visit France with Mr. Johnson and Fuseli. Her friends were, however, unable to accompany her, so she went alone in the December of 1792, chiefly with the object of perfecting her French. Godwin states, though apparently in error, that Fuseli was the cause of her going to France, the acquaintance with the painter having grown into something warmer than mere friendship. Fuseli, however, had a wife and was happily married, so Mary "prudently resolved to retire into another country, far remote from the object who had unintentionally excited the tender passion in her breast."

She certainly arrived in Paris at a dramatic moment; she wrote on December 24 to her sister Everina: "The day after to-morrow I expect to see the King at the bar, and the consequences that will follow I am almost afraid to anticipate." On the day in question, the 26th, Louis XVI. appeared in the Hall of the Convention to plead his cause through his advocate, Desize, and on the same day she wrote that letter to Mr. Johnson which has so often been quoted: "About nine o'clock this morning," she says, "the King passed by my window, moving silently along (excepting now and then a few strokes on the drum, which rendered the stillness more awful) through empty streets, surrounded by the national guards, who, clustering round the carriage, seemed to deserve their name. The inhabitants flocked to their windows, but the casements were all shut, not a voice was heard, nor did I see anything like an insulting gesture. For the first time since I entered France I bowed to the majesty of the people, and respected the propriety of behaviour so perfectly in unison with my own feelings. I can scarcely tell you why, but an association of ideas made the tears flow insensibly from my eyes, when I saw Louis sitting, with more dignity than I expected from his character, in a hackney coach, going to meet death, where so many of his race had triumphed. My fancy instantly brought Louis XIV. before me, entering the capital with all his pomp, after one of his victories so flattering to his pride, only to see the sunshine of prosperity overshadowed by the sublime gloom of misery...."

From an engraving by Ridley, dated 1796, after a painting by John Opie, R.A.

MARY WOLLSTONECRAFT

This picture was purchased for the National Gallery at the sale of the late Mr. William Russell. The reason for supposing that it represents Mary Wollstonecraft rests solely on testimony of the engraving in the Monthly Mirror (published during her lifetime), from which this reproduction was made. Mrs. Merritt made an etching of the picture for Mr. Kegan Paul's edition of the "Letters to Imlay."

Mary first went to stay at the house of Madame Filiettaz, the daughter of Madame Bregantz, in whose school at Putney both Mrs. Bishop and Everina Wollstonecraft had been teachers. Mary was now something of a celebrity—"Authorship," she writes, "is a heavy weight for female shoulders, especially in the sunshine of prosperity"—and she carried with her letters of introduction to several influential people in Paris. She renewed her acquaintance with Tom Paine, became intimate with Helen Maria Williams (who is said to have once lived with Imlay), and visited, among others, the house of Mr. Thomas Christie. It was her intention to go to Switzerland, but there was some trouble about her passport, so she settled at Neuilly, then a village three miles from Paris. "Her habitation here," says Godwin, "was a solitary house in the midst of a garden, with no other habitant than herself and the gardener, an old man who performed for her many offices of a domestic, and would sometimes contend for the honour of making her bed. The gardener had a great veneration for his guest, and would set before her, when alone, some grapes of a particularly fine sort, which she could not without the greatest difficulty obtain of him when she had any person with her as a visitor. Here it was that she conceived, and for the most part executed, her historical and moral view of the French Revolution, into which she incorporated most of the observations she had collected for her letters, and which was written with more sobriety and cheerfulness than the tone in which they had been commenced. In the evening she was accustomed to refresh herself by a walk in a neighbouring wood, from which her host in vain endeavoured to dissuade her, by recounting divers horrible robberies and murders that had been committed there."

It is probable that in March 1793 Mary Wollstonecraft first saw Gilbert Imlay. The meeting occurred at Mr. Christie's house, and her immediate impression was one of dislike, so that on subsequent occasions she avoided him. However, her regard for him rapidly changed into friendship, and later into love. Gilbert Imlay was born in New Jersey about 1755. He served as a captain in the American army during the Revolutionary war, and was the author of "A Topographical Description of the Western Territory of North America," 1792, and a novel entitled "The Emigrants," 1793. In the latter work, as an American, he proposes to "place a mirror to the view of Englishmen, that they may behold the decay of these features that were once so lovely," and further "to prevent the sacrilege which the present practice of matrimonial engagements necessarily produce." It is not known whether these views regarding marriage preceded, or were the result of, his connexion with Mary Wollstonecraft. In 1793 he was engaged in business, probably in the timber trade with Sweden and Norway.

In deciding to devote herself to Imlay, Mary sought no advice and took no one into her confidence. She was evidently deeply in love with him, and felt that their mutual confidence shared by no one else gave a sacredness to their union. Godwin, who is our chief authority on the Imlay episode, states that "the origin of the connexion was about the middle of April 1793, and it was carried on in a private manner for about three months." Imlay had no property whatever, and Mary had objected to marry him, because she would not burden him with her own debts, or "involve him in certain family embarrassments," for which she believed herself responsible. She looked upon her connexion with Imlay, however, "as of the most inviolable nature." Then the French Government passed a decree that all British subjects resident in France should go to prison until a general declaration of peace. It therefore became expedient, not that a marriage should take place, for that would necessitate Mary declaring her nationality, but that she should take the name of Imlay, "which," says Godwin, "from the nature of their connexion (formed on her part at least, with no capricious or fickle design), she conceived herself entitled to do, and obtain a certificate from the American Ambassador, as the wife of a native of that country. Their engagement being thus avowed, they thought proper to reside under the same roof, and for that purpose removed to Paris."

In a letter from Mary Wollstonecraft to her sister Everina, dated from Havre, March 10, 1794, she describes the climate of France as "uncommonly fine," and praises the common people for their manners; but she is also saddened by the scenes that she had witnessed and adds that "death and misery, in every shape of terror, haunt this devoted country.... If any of the many letters I have written have come to your hands or Eliza's, you know that I am safe, through the protection of an American, a most worthy man who joins to uncommon tenderness of heart and quickness of feeling, a soundness of understanding, and reasonableness of temper rarely to be met with. Having been brought up in the interior parts of America, he is a most natural, unaffected creature."

Mary has expressed in the "Rights of Woman" her ideal of the relations between man and wife; she now looked forward to such a life of domestic happiness as she had cherished for some time. She had known much unhappiness in the past. Godwin says: "She brought in the present instance, a wounded and sick heart, to take refuge in the attachment of a chosen friend. Let it not, however, be imagined, that she brought a heart, querulous, and ruined in its taste for pleasure. No; her whole character seemed to change with a change of fortune. Her sorrows, the depression of her spirits, were forgotten, and she assumed all the simplicity and the vivacity of a youthful mind. She was playful, full of confidence, kindness, and sympathy. Her eyes assumed new lustre, and her cheeks new colour and smoothness. Her voice became cheerful; her temper overflowing with universal kindness; and that smile of bewitching tenderness from day to day illuminated her countenance, which all who knew her will so well recollect, and which won, both heart and soul, the affections of almost every one that beheld it." She had now met the man to whom she earnestly believed she could surrender herself with entire devotion. Naturally of an affectionate nature, for the first time in her life, with her impulsive Irish spirit, as Godwin says, "she gave way to all the sensibilities of her nature."

The affair was nevertheless doomed to failure from the first. Mary had taken her step without much forethought. She attributed to Imlay "uncommon tenderness of heart," but she did not detect his instability of character. He certainly fascinated her, as he fascinated other women, both before and after his attachment to Mary. He was not the man to be satisfied with one woman as his life-companion. A typical American, he was deeply immersed in business, but his affairs may not have claimed as much of his time as he represented. In the September after he set up house with Mary, that is in '93, the year of the Terror, he left her in Paris while he went to Havre, formerly known as Havre de Grace, but then altered to Havre Marat. It is awful to think what must have been the life of this lonely stranger in Paris at such a time. Yet her letters to Imlay contain hardly a reference to the events of the Revolution.

Mary, tired of waiting for Imlay's return to Paris, and sickened with the "growing cruelties of Robespierre," joined him at Havre in January 1794, and on May 14 she gave birth to a girl, whom she named Frances in memory of Fanny Blood, the friend of her youth. There is every evidence throughout her letters to Imlay of how tenderly she loved the little one. In a letter to Everina, dated from Paris on September 20, she speaks thus of little Fanny:

"I want you to see my little girl, who is more like a boy. She is ready to fly away with spirits, and has eloquent health in her cheeks and eyes. She does not promise to be a beauty, but appears wonderfully intelligent, and though I am sure she has her father's quick temper and feelings, her good humour runs away with all the credit of my good nursing."

In September Imlay left Havre for London, and now that the Terror had subsided Mary returned to Paris. This separation really meant the end of their camaraderie. They were to meet again, but never on the old footing. The journey proved the most fatiguing that she ever made, the carriage in which she travelled breaking down four times between Havre and Paris. Imlay promised to come to Paris in the course of two months, and she expected him till the end of the year with cheerfulness. With the press of business and other distractions his feelings for her and the child had cooled, as the tone of his letters betrayed. For three months longer Imlay put her off with unsatisfactory explanations, but her suspense came to an end in April, when she went to London at his request. Her gravest forebodings proved too true. Imlay was already living with a young actress belonging to a company of strolling players; and it was evident, though at first he protested to the contrary, that Mary was only a second consideration in his life. He provided her, however, with a furnished house, and she did not at once abandon hope of a reconciliation: but when she realised that hope was useless, in her despair she resolved to take her life. Whether she actually attempted suicide, or whether Imlay learnt of her intention in time to prevent her, is not actually known. Imlay was at this time engaged in trade with Norway, and requiring a trustworthy representative to transact some confidential business, it was thought that the journey would restore Mary's health and spirits. She therefore consented to take the voyage, and set out early in April 1795, with a document drawn up by Imlay appointing her as his representative, and describing her as "Mary Imlay, my best friend, and wife," and concluding: "Thus, confiding in the talent, zeal, and earnestness of my dearly beloved friend and companion; I submit the management of these affairs entirely and implicitly to her discretion: Remaining most sincerely and affectionately hers truly, G. Imlay."

The letters describing her travels, excluding any personal matters, were issued in 1796, as "Letters from Sweden and Norway," one of her most readable books. The portions eliminated from these letters were printed by Godwin in his wife's posthumous works, and are given in the present volume. She returned to England early in October with a heavy heart. Imlay had promised to meet her on the homeward journey, possibly at Hamburg, and to take her to Switzerland, but she hastened to London to find her suspicions confirmed. He provided her with a lodging, but entirely neglected her for some woman with whom he was living. On first making the discovery of his fresh intrigue, and in her agony of mind, she sought Imlay at the house he had furnished for his new companion. The conference resulted in her utter despair, and she decided to drown herself. She first went to Battersea Bridge, but found too many people there; and therefore walked on to Putney. It was night and raining when she arrived there, and after wandering up and down the bridge for half-an-hour until her clothing was thoroughly drenched she threw herself into the river. She was, however, rescued from the water and, although unconscious, her life was saved.

Mary met Imlay casually on two or three other occasions; probably her last sight of him was in the New Road (now Marylebone Road), when "he alighted from his horse, and walked with her some time; and the re-encounter passed," she assured Godwin, "without producing in her any oppressive emotion." Mary refused to accept any pecuniary assistance for herself from Imlay, but he gave a bond for a sum to be settled on her, the interest to be devoted to the maintenance of their child; neither principal nor interest, however, was ever paid. What ultimately became of Imlay is not known.

Mary at length resigned herself to the inevitable. Her old friend and publisher, Mr. Johnson, came to her aid, and she resolved to resume her literary work for the support of herself and her child. She was once more seen in literary society. Among the people whom she met at this time was William Godwin. Three years her senior, he was one of the most advanced republicans of the time, the author of "Political Justice" and the novel "Caleb Williams." They had met before, for the first time in November 1791, but she displeased Godwin, because her vivacious gossip silenced the naturally quiet Thomas Paine, whom he was anxious to hear talk. Although they met occasionally afterwards, it was not until 1796 that they became friendly. There must have been something about Godwin that made him extremely attractive to his friends, for he numbered among them some of the most charming women of the day, and such men as Wordsworth, Lamb, Hazlitt, and Shelley were proud to be of his circle. To the members of his family he was of a kind, even affectionate, disposition. Unfortunately, he appears to the worst advantage—a kind of early Pecksniff—in his later correspondence and relations with Shelley, and it is by this correspondence at the present day that he is best known. The fine side-face portrait of Godwin by Northcote, in the National Portrait Gallery, preserves for us all the beauty of his intellectual brow and eyes. Another portrait of Godwin, full-face, with a long sad nose, by Pickersgill, once to be seen in the National Portrait Gallery, is not so pleasing. In a letter to Cottle, Southey gives an unflattering portrait of Godwin at the time of his marriage, which seems to suggest the full-face portrait of the philosopher—"he has large noble eyes, and a nose—oh, most abominable nose! Language is not vituperatious enough to describe the effect of its downward elongation."

Godwin describes his courtship with Mary as "friendship melting into love." They agreed to live together, but Godwin took rooms about twenty doors from their home in the Polygon, Somers Town, as it was one of his theories that living together under the same roof is destructive of family happiness. Godwin went to his rooms as soon as he rose in the morning, generally without taking breakfast with Mary, and he sometimes slept at his lodgings. They rarely met again until dinner-time, unless to take a walk together. During the day this extraordinary couple would communicate with each other by means of short letters or notes. Mr. Kegan Paul prints some of these; such as Godwin's:

"I will have the honour to dine with you. You ask me whether I can get you four orders. I do not know, but I do not think the thing impossible. How do you do?"

And Mary's: "Fanny is delighted with the thought of dining with you. But I wish you to eat your meat first, and let her come up with the pudding. I shall probably knock at your door on my way to Opie's; but should I not find you, let me request you not to be too late this evening. Do not give Fanny butter with her pudding." This note is dated April 20, 1797, and probably fixes the time when Mary was sitting for her portrait to Opie.

On the whole, Godwin and Mary lived happily together, with very occasional clouds, mainly due to her over-sensitive nature, and his confirmed bachelor habits.

Although both were opposed to matrimony on principle, they were married at Old St. Pancras Church on March 29, 1797, the clerk of the church being witness. Godwin does not mention the event in his carefully registered diary. The reason for the marriage was that Mary was about to become a mother, and it was for the sake of the child that they deemed it prudent to go through the ceremony. But it was not made public at once, chiefly for fear that Johnson should cease to help Mary. Mrs. Inchbald and Mrs. Reveley, two of Godwin's admirers, were so upset at the announcement of his marriage that they shed tears.

An interesting description of Mary at this time is given in Southey's letter to Cottle, quoted above, dated March 13, 1797. He says, "Of all the lions or literati I have seen here, Mary Imlay's countenance is the best, infinitely the best: the only fault in it is an expression somewhat similar to what the prints of Horne Tooke display—an expression indicating superiority; not haughtiness, not sarcasm, in Mary Imlay, but still it is unpleasant. Her eyes are light brown, and although the lid of one of them is affected by a little paralysis, they are the most meaning I ever saw."

Mary busied herself with literary work; otherwise her short married life was uneventful. Godwin made a journey with his friend Basil Montagu to Staffordshire from June 3 to 20, and the correspondence between husband and wife during this time, which Mr. Paul prints, is most delightful reading, and shows how entirely in sympathy they were.

From a photo by Emery, Walker after the picture by Opie (probably painted in April, 1797) in the National Portrait Gallery.

MARY WOLLSTONECRAFT

This picture passed from Godwin's hands on his death to his grandson, Sir Percy Florence Shelley. It was afterwards bequeathed to the nation by his widow, Lady Shelley. It was engraved by Heath (Jan. 1, 1798) for Godwin's memoir of his wife. An engraving of it also appeared in the Lady's Magazine, from which the frontispiece to this book was made, and a mezzotint by W. T. Annis was published in 1802. Mrs. Merritt also made an etching of the picture for Mr. Paul's edition of the "Letters to Imlay."

On August 30, Mary's child was born, not the William so much desired by them both but Mary, who afterwards became Mrs. Shelley. All seemed well with the mother until September 3, when alarming symptoms appeared. The best medical advice was obtained, but after a week's illness, on Sunday morning, the 10th, at twenty minutes to eight, she sank and died. During her illness, when in great agony, an anodyne was administered, which gave Mary some relief, when she exclaimed, "Oh, Godwin, I am in heaven." But, as Mr. Kegan Paul says, "even at that moment Godwin declined to be entrapped into the admission that heaven existed," and his instant reply was: "You mean, my dear, that your physical sensations are somewhat easier." Mary Godwin, however, did not share her husband's religious doubts. Her sufferings had been great, but her death was a peaceful one.

Godwin's grief was very deep, as the letters that he wrote immediately after her death, and his tribute to her memory in the "Memoirs" testify. Mary Godwin was buried in Old St. Pancras churchyard on September 15, in the presence of most of her friends. Godwin lived till 1836, when he was laid beside her. Many years afterwards, at the same graveside, Shelley is said to have plighted his troth to Mary Godwin's daughter. In 1851, when the Metropolitan and Midland Railways were constructed at St. Pancras, the graveyard was destroyed, but the bodies of Mary and William Godwin were removed by their grandson, Sir Percy Shelley, to Bournemouth, where they now rest with his remains, and those of his mother, Mrs. Shelley.

In the year following Mary's death (1798) Godwin edited his wife's "Posthumous Works," in four volumes, in which appeared the letters to Imlay, and her incomplete novel "The Wrongs of Woman." His tribute to Mary Godwin's memory was also published in 1798, under the title of "Memoirs of the Author of A Vindication of the Rights of Woman." Godwin's novel, "St. Leon" came out in 1799; his tragedy "Antonio" was produced only to fail, in 1800, and in 1801, he was wooed and won by Mrs. Clairmont, a widow. The Godwin household was a somewhat mixed one, consisting, as it did, of Fanny Imlay, Mary Godwin, Mrs. Godwin's two children, Charles and Claire Clairmont, and also of William, the only child born of her marriage with Godwin. In 1812 Shelley began a correspondence with Godwin, which ultimately led to Mary Godwin's elopement with the poet. Poor Fanny Imlay, or Godwin, as she was called after her mother's death, died at the age of nineteen by her own hand, in October 1816. Her life had been far from happy in this strange household. She had grown to love Shelley, but his choice had fallen on her half-sister, so she bravely kept her secret to herself. One day she suddenly left home and travelled to Swansea, where she was found lying dead the morning after her arrival, in the inn where she had taken a room, "her long brown hair about her face; a bottle of laudanum upon the table, and a note which ran thus: 'I have long determined that the best thing I could do was to put an end to the existence of a being whose birth was unfortunate, and whose life has only been a series of pain to those persons who have hurt their health in endeavouring to promote her welfare.' She had with her the little Genevan watch, a gift of travel from Mary and Shelley: and in her purse were a few shillings."[1]

Shelley, afterwards recalling his last interview with Fanny in London, wrote this stanza:

"Her voice did quiver as we parted;
Yet knew I not that heart was broken
From whence it came, and I departed
Heeding not the words then spoken.
Misery—O Misery,
This world is all too wide for thee!"

III

The vicissitudes to which Mary Wollstonecraft was so largely a prey during her lifetime seem to have pursued her after death. In her own day recognised as a public character, reviled by most of her contemporaries in terms not less ungentle than Horace Walpole's epithets, "a hyena in petticoats" or "a philosophising serpent," posterity has proved hardly more lenient to her. But the vigorous work of this "female patriot" has saved her name from that descent into obscurity which is the reward of many men and women more talented than Mary Wollstonecraft. Reputed chiefly as an unsexed being, who had written "A Vindication of the Rights of Women," she was not the first woman to hold views on the emancipation of her sex; but her chief crimes were in expressing them for the instruction of the public, and having the courage to live up to her opinions. Whether right or wrong, she paid the penalty of violating custom by discussing forbidden subjects. It is true that she detected many social evils, and suggested some excellent remedies for their amelioration, but the time was not ripe for her book, and she suffered the usual fate of the pioneer. Moreover, her memoir by William Godwin, beautiful as it is in many respects, exercised a distinctly harmful influence in regard to her memory. The very fact that she became the wife of so notorious a man, was sufficient reason to condemn her in the eyes of her countrymen.

For two generations after her death practically no attempt was made to remove the stigma from her name. But at length the late Mr. Kegan Paul, a man of wide and generous sympathies, made a serious effort to obtain something like justice for Mary Wollstonecraft. In his book on William Godwin, published in 1876, the true story of Mary's life was told for the first time. It was somewhat of a revelation, for it recorded the history of an unhappy but brave and loyal woman, whose faults proceeded from excessive sensibility and from a heart that was over-susceptible. Mary Wollstonecraft was an idealist in a very matter-of-fact age, and her outlook on life, like that of most idealists, was strongly affected by her imagination. She saw people and events in brilliant lights or sombre shadows— it was a power akin to enthusiasm which enabled her to produce some of her best writing, but it also prevented her from seeing the defects of her worst work. Since Mr. Kegan Paul's memoir, Mary Wollstonecraft has been viewed from an entirely different aspect, and many there are who have come under the spell of her fascinating personality. It is not, however, her message alone that now interests us, but the woman herself, her desires, her aspirations, her struggles, and her love. Pathetic and lonely, she stands out in the faint mists of the past, a woman that will continue to evoke sympathy when her books are no longer read. But it is safe to predict that the pages reprinted in this volume are not destined to share the fate of the rest of her work. Other writers have been unhappy and have known the pains of unrequited love, but Mary Wollstonecraft addressed these letters with a breaking heart to the man whom she adored, the most passionate love letters in our literature. It is true that she was a votary of Rousseau, and that she had probably assimilated from the study of his work not only many of his views, but something of his style; it does not, however, appear that she had any motive in writing these letters other than to plead her cause with Imlay. She was far too sensitive to have intended them for publication, and it was only by a mere chance that they were rescued from oblivion.

December 1907.

LETTERS TO GILBERT IMLAY

LETTER I

Two o'Clock [Paris, June 1793].

My dear love, after making my arrangements for our snug dinner to-day, I have been taken by storm, and obliged to promise to dine, at an early hour, with the Miss —s, the only day they intend to pass here. I shall however leave the key in the door, and hope to find you at my fire-side when I return, about eight o'clock. Will you not wait for poor Joan?—whom you will find better, and till then think very affectionately of her.

Yours, truly,

MARY.

I am sitting down to dinner; so do not send an answer.

LETTER II

Past Twelve o'Clock, Monday Night [Paris, Aug. 1793].

I obey an emotion of my heart, which made me think of wishing thee, my love, good-night! before I go to rest, with more tenderness than I can to-morrow, when writing a hasty line or two under Colonel —'s eye. You can scarcely imagine with what pleasure I anticipate the day, when we are to begin almost to live together; and you would smile to hear how many plans of employment I have in my head, now that I am confident my heart has found peace in your bosom.—Cherish me with that dignified tenderness, which I have only found in you; and your own dear girl will try to keep under a quickness of feeling, that has sometimes given you pain.—Yes, I will be good, that I may deserve to be happy; and whilst you love me, I cannot again fall into the miserable state, which rendered life a burthen almost too heavy to be borne.

But, good-night!—God bless you! Sterne says, that is equal to a kiss—yet I would rather give you the kiss into the bargain, glowing with gratitude to Heaven, and affection to you. I like the word affection, because it signifies something habitual; and we are soon to meet, to try whether we have mind enough to keep our hearts warm.

MARY.

I will be at the barrier a little after ten o'clock to-morrow.[2]—Yours—

LETTER III

Wednesday Morning [Paris, Aug. 1793].

You have often called me, dear girl, but you would now say good, did you know how very attentive I have been to the — ever since I came to Paris. I am not however going to trouble you with the account, because I like to see your eyes praise me; and Milton insinuates, that, during such recitals, there are interruptions, not ungrateful to the heart, when the honey that drops from the lips is not merely words.

Yet, I shall not (let me tell you before these people enter, to force me to huddle away my letter) be content with only a kiss of DUTY—you must be glad to see me—because you are glad—or I will make love to the shade of Mirabeau, to whom my heart continually turned, whilst I was talking with Madame

—, forcibly telling me, that it will ever have sufficient warmth to love, whether I will or not, sentiment, though I so highly respect principle.—

Not that I think Mirabeau utterly devoid of principles—Far from it—and, if I had not begun to form a new theory respecting men, I should, in the vanity of my heart, have imagined that I could have made something of his—it was composed of such materials—Hush! here they come—and love flies away in the twinkling of an eye, leaving a little brush of his wing on my pale cheeks.

I hope to see Dr. — this morning; I am going to Mr. —'s to meet him. —, and some others, are invited to dine with us to-day; and to-morrow I am to spend the day with —.

I shall probably not be able to return to — to-morrow; but it is no matter, because I must take a carriage, I have so many books, that I immediately want, to take with me.—On Friday then I shall expect you to dine with me—and, if you come a little before dinner, it is so long since I have seen you, you will not be scolded by yours affectionately,

MARY.

LETTER IV

Friday Morning [Paris, Sept. 1793].

A man, whom a letter from Mr. — previously announced, called here yesterday for the payment of a draft; and, as he seemed disappointed at not finding you at home, I sent him to Mr. —. I have since seen him, and he tells me that he has settled the business.

So much for business!—May I venture to talk a little longer about less weighty affairs?—How are you?—I have been following you all along the road this comfortless weather; for, when I am absent from those I love, my imagination is as lively, as if my senses had never been gratified by their presence—I was going to say caresses—and why should I not? I have found out that I have more mind than you, in one respect; because I can, without any violent effort of reason, find food for love in the same object, much longer than you can.—The way to my senses is through my heart; but, forgive me! I think there is sometimes a shorter cut to yours.

With ninety-nine men out of a hundred, a very sufficient dash of folly is necessary to render a woman piquante, a soft word for desirable; and, beyond these casual ebullitions of sympathy, few look for enjoyment by fostering a passion in their hearts. One reason, in short, why I wish my whole sex to become wiser, is, that the foolish ones may not, by their pretty folly, rob those whose sensibility keeps down their vanity, of the few roses that afford them some solace in the thorny road of life.

I do not know how I fell into these reflections, excepting one thought produced it—that these continual separations were necessary to warm your affection.—Of late, we are always separating.—Crack!—crack!—and away you go.—This joke wears the sallow cast of thought; for, though I began to write cheerfully, some melancholy tears have found their way into my eyes, that linger there, whilst a glow of tenderness at my heart whispers that you are one of the best creatures in the world.—Pardon then the vagaries of a mind, that has been almost "crazed by care," as well as "crossed in hapless love," and bear with me a little longer!—When we are settled in the country together, more duties will open before me, and my heart, which now, trembling into peace, is agitated by every emotion that awakens the remembrance of old griefs, will learn to rest on yours, with that dignity your character, not to talk of my own, demands.

Take care of yourself—and write soon to your own girl (you may add dear, if you please) who sincerely loves you, and will try to convince you of it, by becoming happier.

MARY.

LETTER V

Sunday Night [Paris, 1793].

I have just received your letter, and feel as if I could not go to bed tranquilly without saying a few words in reply—merely to tell you, that my mind is serene and my heart affectionate.

Ever since you last saw me inclined to faint, I have felt some gentle twitches, which make me begin to think, that I am nourishing a creature who will soon be sensible of my care.—This thought has not only produced an overflowing of tenderness to you, but made me very attentive to calm my mind and take exercise, lest I should destroy an object, in whom we are to have a mutual interest, you know. Yesterday—do not smile!—finding that I had hurt myself by lifting precipitately a large log of wood, I sat down in an agony, till I felt those said twitches again.

Are you very busy?

So you may reckon on its being finished soon, though not before you come home, unless you are detained longer than I now allow myself to believe you will.—

Be that as it may, write to me, my best love, and bid me be patient—kindly—and the expressions of kindness will again beguile the time, as sweetly as they have done to-night.—Tell me also over and over again, that your happiness (and you deserve to be happy!) is closely connected with mine, and I will try to dissipate, as they rise, the fumes of former discontent, that have too often clouded the sunshine, which you have endeavoured to diffuse through my mind. God bless you! Take care of yourself, and remember with tenderness your affectionate

MARY.

I am going to rest very happy, and you have made me so.—This is the kindest good-night I can utter.

LETTER VI

Friday Morning [Paris, Dec. 1793].

I am glad to find that other people can be unreasonable, as well as myself—for be it known to thee, that I answered thy first letter, the very night it reached me (Sunday), though thou couldst not receive it before Wednesday, because it was not sent off till the next day.—There is a full, true, and particular account.—

Yet I am not angry with thee, my love, for I think that it is a proof of stupidity, and likewise of a milk-and-water affection, which comes to the same thing, when the temper is governed by a square and compass.—There is nothing picturesque in this straight-lined equality, and the passions always give grace to the actions.

Recollection now makes my heart bound to thee; but, it is not to thy money-getting face, though I cannot be seriously displeased with the exertion which increases my esteem, or rather is what I should have expected from thy character.—No; I have thy honest countenance before me—Pop—relaxed by tenderness; a little—little wounded by my whims; and thy eyes glistening with sympathy.—Thy lips then feel softer than soft—and I rest my cheek on thine, forgetting all the world.—I have not left the hue of love out of the picture—the rosy glow; and fancy has spread it over my own cheeks, I believe, for I feel them burning, whilst a delicious tear trembles in my eye, that would be all your own, if a grateful emotion directed to the Father of nature, who has made me thus alive to happiness, did not give more warmth to the sentiment it divides—I must pause a moment.

Need I tell you that I am tranquil after writing thus?—I do not know why, but I have more confidence in your affection, when absent, than present; nay, I think that you must love me, for, in the sincerity of my heart let me say it, I believe I deserve your tenderness, because I am true, and have a degree of sensibility that you can see and relish.

Yours sincerely,
MARY.

LETTER VII

Sunday Morning [Paris, Dec. 29, 1793].

You seem to have taken up your abode at Havre. Pray sir! when do you think of coming home? or, to write very considerately, when will business permit you? I shall expect (as the country people say in England) that you will make a power of money to indemnify me for your absence.

Well! but, my love, to the old story—am I to see you this week, or this month?—I do not know what you are about—for, as you did not tell me, I would not ask Mr. —, who is generally pretty communicative.

I long to see Mrs. —; not to hear from you, so do not give yourself airs, but to get a letter from Mr. —. And I am half angry with you for not informing me whether she had brought one with her or not.—On this score I will cork up some of the kind things that were ready to drop from my pen, which has never been dipt in gall when addressing you; or, will only suffer an exclamation—"The creature!" or a kind look to escape me, when I pass the slippers—which I could not remove from my falle door, though they are not the handsomest of their kind.

Be not too anxious to get money!—for nothing worth having is to be purchased. God bless you.

Yours affectionately,

MARY.

Monday Night [Paris, Dec. 30, 1793].

My best love, your letter to-night was particularly grateful to my heart, depressed by the letters I received by —, for he brought me several, and the parcel of books directed to Mr. — was for me. Mr. — 's letter was long and very affectionate; but the account he gives me of his own affairs, though he obviously makes the best of them, has vexed me.

A melancholy letter from my sister — has also harrassed my mind—that from my brother would have given me sincere pleasure; but for

There is a spirit of independence in his letter, that will please you; and you shall see it, when we are once more over the fire together.—I think that you would hail him as a brother, with one of your tender looks, when your heart not only gives a lustre to your eye, but a dance of playfulness, that he would meet with a glow half made up of bashfulness, and a desire to please the—where shall I find a word to express the relationship which subsists between us?—Shall I ask the little twitcher?—But I have dropt half the sentence that was to tell you how much he would be inclined to love the man loved by his sister. I have been fancying myself sitting between you, ever since I began to write, and my heart has leaped at the thought! You see how I chat to you.

I did not receive your letter till I came home; and I did not expect it, for the post came in much later than usual. It was a cordial to me—and I wanted one.

Mr. — tells me that he has written again and again.—Love him a little!—It would be a kind of separation, if you did not love those I love.

There was so much considerate tenderness in your epistle to-night, that, if it has not made you dearer to me, it has made me forcibly feel how very dear you are to me, by charming away half my cares.

Yours affectionately.

MARY.

Tuesday Morning [Paris, Dec. 31, 1793].

Though I have just sent a letter off, yet, as captain — offers to take one, I am not willing to let him go without a kind greeting, because trifles of this sort, without having any effect on my mind, damp my spirits:—and you, with all your struggles to be manly, have some of his same sensibility.—Do not bid it begone, for I love to see it striving to master your features; besides, these kind of sympathies are the life of affection: and why, in cultivating our understandings, should we try to dry up these springs of pleasure, which gush out to give a freshness to days browned by care!

The books sent to me are such as we may read together; so I shall not look into them till you return; when you shall read, whilst I mend my stockings.

Yours truly,

MARY.

Wednesday Night [Paris, Jan. 1, 1794].

As I have been, you tell me, three days without writing, I ought not to complain of two: yet, as I expected to receive a letter this afternoon, I am hurt; and why should I, by concealing it, affect the heroism I do not feel?

I hate commerce. How differently must —'s head and heart be organized from mine! You will tell me, that exertions are necessary: I am weary of them! The face of things, public and private, vexes me. The "peace" and clemency which seemed to be dawning a few days ago, disappear again. "I am fallen," as Milton said, "on evil days;" for I really believe that Europe will be in a state of convulsion, during half a century at least. Life is but a labour of patience: it is always rolling a great stone up a hill; for, before a person can find a resting-place, imagining it is lodged, down it comes again, and all the work is to be done over anew!

Should I attempt to write any more, I could not change the strain. My head aches, and my heart is heavy. The world appears an "unweeded garden," where "things rank and vile" flourish best.

If you do not return soon—or, which is no such mighty matter, talk of it—I will throw your slippers out at window, and be off—nobody knows where.

MARY.

Finding that I was observed, I told the good women, the two Mrs. —s, simply that I was with child: and let them stare! and —, and —, nay, all the world, may know it for aught I care!—Yet I wish to avoid —'s coarse jokes.

Considering the care and anxiety a woman must have about a child before it comes into the world, it seems to me, by a natural right, to belong to her. When men get immersed in the world, they seem to lose all sensations, excepting those necessary to continue or produce life!—Are these the privileges of reason? Amongst the feathered race, whilst the hen keeps the young warm, her mate stays by to cheer her; but it is sufficient for man to condescend to get a child, in order to claim it.—A man is a tyrant!

You may now tell me, that, if it were not for me, you would be laughing away with some honest fellows in London. The casual exercise of social sympathy would not be sufficient for me—I should not think such an heartless life worth preserving.—It is necessary to be in good-humour with you, to be pleased with the world.

Thursday Morning [Paris, Jan. 2, 1794].

I was very low-spirited last night, ready to quarrel with your cheerful temper, which makes absence easy to you.—And, why should I mince the matter? I was offended at your not even mentioning it—I do not want to be loved like a goddess but I wish to be necessary to you. God bless you![4]

LETTER XI

Monday Night [Paris, Jan. 1794].

I have just received your kind and rational letter, and would fain hide my face, glowing with shame for my folly.—I would hide it in your bosom, if you would again open it to me, and nestle closely till you bade my fluttering heart be still, by saying that you forgave me. With eyes overflowing with tears, and in the humblest attitude, I entreat you.—Do not turn from me, for indeed I love you fondly, and have been very wretched, since the night I was so cruelly hurt by thinking that you had no confidence in me—

It is time for me to grow more reasonable, a few more of these caprices of sensibility would destroy me. I have, in fact, been very much indisposed for a few days past, and the notion that I was tormenting, or perhaps killing, a poor little animal, about whom I am grown anxious and tender, now I feel it alive, made me worse. My bowels have been dreadfully disordered, and every thing I ate or drank disagreed with my stomach; still I feel intimations of its existence, though they have been fainter.

Do you think that the creature goes regularly to sleep? I am ready to ask as many questions as Voltaire's Man of Forty Crowns. Ah! do not continue to be angry with me! You perceive that I am already smiling through my tears—You have lightened my heart, and my frozen spirits are melting into playfulness.

Write the moment you receive this. I shall count the minutes. But drop not an angry word—I cannot now bear it. Yet, if you think I deserve a scolding (it does not admit of a question, I grant), wait till you come back—and then, if you are angry one day, I shall be sure of seeing you the next.

— did not write to you, I suppose, because he talked of going to Havre. Hearing that I was ill, he called very kindly on me, not dreaming that it was some words that he incautiously let fall, which rendered me so.

God bless you, my love; do not shut your heart against a return of tenderness; and, as I now in fancy cling to you, be more than ever my support.—Feel but as affectionate when you read this letter, as I did writing it, and you will make happy your

MARY.

Wednesday Morning [Paris, Jan. 1794].

I will never, if I am not entirely cured of quarrelling, begin to encourage "quick-coming fancies," when we are separated. Yesterday, my love, I could not open your letter for some time; and, though it was not half as severe as I merited, it threw me into such a fit of trembling, as seriously alarmed me. I did not, as you may suppose, care for a little pain on my own account; but all the fears which I have had for a few days past, returned with fresh force. This morning I am better; will you not be glad to hear it? You perceive that sorrow has almost made a child of me, and that I want to be soothed to peace.

One thing you mistake in my character, and imagine that to be coldness which is just the contrary. For, when I am hurt by the person most dear to me, I must let out a whole torrent of emotions, in which tenderness would be uppermost, or stifle them altogether; and it appears to me almost a duty to stifle them, when I imagine that I am treated with coldness.

I am afraid that I have vexed you, my own [Imlay]. I know the quickness of your feelings—and let me, in the sincerity of my heart, assure you, there is nothing I would not suffer to make you happy. My own happiness wholly depends on you—and, knowing you, when my reason is not clouded, I look forward to a rational prospect of as much felicity as the earth affords—with a little dash of rapture into the bargain, if you will look at me, when we work again, as you have sometimes greeted, your humbled, yet most affectionate

MARY.

Thursday Night [Paris, Jan. 1794].

I have been wishing the time away, my kind love, unable to rest till I knew that my penitential letter had reached your hand—and this afternoon, when your tender epistle of Tuesday gave such exquisite pleasure to your poor sick girl, her heart smote her to think that you were still to receive another cold one.—Burn it also, my [Imlay]; yet do not forget that even those letters were full of love; and I shall ever recollect, that you did not wait to be mollified by my penitence, before you took me again to your heart.

I have been unwell, and would not, now I am recovering, take a journey, because I have been seriously alarmed and angry with myself, dreading continually the fatal consequence of my folly.—But, should you think it right to remain at Havre, I shall find some opportunity, in the course of a fortnight, or less perhaps, to come to you, and before then I shall be strong again.—Yet do not be uneasy! I am really better, and never took such care of myself, as I have done since you restored my peace of mind. The girl is come to warm my bed—so I will tenderly say, good-night! and write a line or two in the morning.

Morning.

I wish you were here to walk with me this fine morning! yet your absence shall not prevent me. I have stayed at home too much; though, when I was so dreadfully out of spirits, I was careless of every thing.

I will now sally forth (you will go with me in my heart) and try whether this fine bracing air will not give the vigour to the poor babe, it had, before I so inconsiderately gave way to the grief that deranged my bowels, and gave a turn to my whole system.

Yours truly

MARY IMLAY.

LETTER XIV

Saturday Morning [Paris, Feb. 1794].

The two or three letters, which I have written to you lately, my love, will serve as an answer to your explanatory one. I cannot but respect your motives and conduct. I always respected them; and was only hurt, by what seemed to me a want of confidence, and consequently affection.—I thought also, that if you were obliged to stay three months at Havre, I might as well have been with you.—Well! well, what signifies what I brooded over—Let us now be friends!

I shall probably receive a letter from you to-day, sealing my pardon—and I will be careful not to torment you with my querulous humours, at least, till I see you again. Act as circumstances direct, and I will not enquire when they will permit you to return, convinced that you will hasten to your Mary, when you have attained (or lost sight of) the object of your journey.

What a picture have you sketched of our fire-side! Yes, my love, my fancy was instantly at work, and I found my head on your shoulder, whilst my eyes were fixed on the little creatures that were clinging about your knees. I did not absolutely determine that there should be six—if you have not set your heart on this round number.

I am going to dine with Mrs. —. I have not been to visit her since the first day she came to Paris. I wish indeed to be out in the air as much as I can; for the exercise I have taken these two or three days past, has been of such service to me, that I hope shortly to tell you, that I am quite well. I have scarcely slept before last night, and then not much.—The two Mrs. —s have been very anxious and tender.

Yours truly

MARY.

I need not desire you to give the colonel a good bottle of wine.

LETTER XV

Sunday Morning [Paris, Feb. 1794].

I wrote to you yesterday, my [Imlay]; but, finding that the colonel is still detained (for his passport was forgotten at the office yesterday) I am not willing to let so many days elapse without your hearing from me, after having talked of illness and apprehensions.

I cannot boast of being quite recovered, yet I am (I must use my Yorkshire phrase; for, when my heart is warm, pop come the expressions of childhood into my head) so lightsome, that I think it will not go badly with me.—And nothing shall be wanting on my part, I assure you; for I am urged on, not only by an enlivened affection for you, but by a new-born tenderness that plays cheerly round my dilating heart.

I was therefore, in defiance of cold and dirt, out in the air the greater part of yesterday; and, if I get over this evening without a return of the fever that has tormented me, I shall talk no more of illness. I have promised the little creature, that its mother, who ought to cherish it, will not again plague it, and begged it to pardon me; and, since I could not hug either it or you to my breast, I have to my heart.—I am afraid to read over this prattle—but it is only for your eye.

I have been seriously vexed, to find that, whilst you were harrassed by impediments in your undertakings, I was giving you additional uneasiness.—If you can make any of your plans answer—it is well, I do not think a little money inconvenient; but, should they fail, we will struggle cheerfully together—drawn closer by the pinching blasts of poverty.

Adieu, my love! Write often to your poor girl, and write long letters; for I not only like them for being longer, but because more heart steals into them; and I am happy to catch your heart whenever I can.

Yours sincerely

MARY.

LETTER XVI

Tuesday Morning [Paris, Feb. 1794].

I seize this opportunity to inform you, that I am to set out on Thursday with Mr. —, and hope to tell you soon (on your lips) how glad I shall be to see you. I have just got my passport, for I do not foresee any impediment to my reaching Havre, to bid you good-night next Friday in my new apartment—where I am to meet you and love, in spite of care, to smile me to sleep—for I have not caught much rest since we parted.

You have, by your tenderness and worth, twisted yourself more artfully round my heart, than I supposed possible.—Let me indulge the thought, that I have thrown out some tendrils to cling to the elm by which I wish to be supported.—This is talking a new language for me!—But, knowing that I am not a parasite-plant, I am willing to receive the proofs of affection, that every pulse replies to, when I think of being once more in the same house with you. God bless you!

Yours truly
MARY.

Wednesday Morning [Paris, Feb. 1794].

I only send this as an avant-coureur, without jack-boots, to tell you, that I am again on the wing, and hope to be with you a few hours after you receive it. I shall find you well, and composed, I am sure; or, more properly speaking, cheerful.—What is the reason that my spirits are not as manageable as yours? Yet, now I think of it, I will not allow that your temper is even, though I have promised myself, in order to obtain my own forgiveness, that I will not ruffle it for a long, long time—I am afraid to say never.

Farewell for a moment!—Do not forget that I am driving towards you in person! My mind, unfettered, has flown to you long since, or rather has never left you.

I am well, and have no apprehension that I shall find the journey too fatiguing, when I follow the lead of my heart.—With my face turned to Havre my spirits will not sink—and my mind has always hitherto enabled my body to do whatever I wished.

Yours affectionately,

MARY.

Thursday Morning, Havre, March 12 [1794].

We are such creatures of habit, my love, that, though I cannot say I was sorry, childishly so, for your going,[5] when I knew that you were to stay such a short time, and I had a plan of employment; yet I could not sleep.—I turned to your side of the bed, and tried to make the most of the comfort of the pillow, which you used to tell me I was churlish about; but all would not do.—I took nevertheless my walk before breakfast, though the weather was not very inviting—and here I am, wishing you a finer day, and seeing you peep over my shoulder, as I write, with one of your kindest looks—when your eyes glisten, and a suffusion creeps over your relaxing features.

But I do not mean to dally with you this morning—So God bless you! Take care of yourself—and sometimes fold to your heart your affectionate

MARY.

[Havre, March, 1794].

Do not call me stupid, for leaving on the table the little bit of paper I was to inclose.—This comes of being in love at the fag-end of a letter of business.—You know, you say, they will not chime together.—I had got you by the fire-side, with the gigot smoking on the board, to lard your poor bare ribs—and behold, I closed my letter without taking the paper up, that was directly under my eyes! What had I got in them to render me so blind?—I give you leave to answer the question, if you will not scold; for I am,

Yours most affectionately,

MARY.

[Havre] Sunday, August 17 [1794].

I have promised — to go with him to his country-house, where he is now permitted to dine—I, and the little darling, to be sure[6]—whom I cannot help kissing with more fondness, since you left us. I think I shall enjoy the fine prospect, and that it will rather enliven, than satiate my imagination.

I have called on Mrs. —. She has the manners of a gentlewoman, with a dash of the easy French coquetry, which renders her piquante.—But Monsieur her husband, whom nature never dreamed of casting in either the mould of a gentleman or lover, makes but an aukward figure in the foreground of the picture.

The H—s are very ugly, without doubt—and the house smelt of commerce from top to toe—so that his abortive attempt to display taste, only proved it to be one of the things not to be bought with gold. I was in a room a moment alone, and my attention was attracted by the pendule—A nymph was offering up her vows before a smoking altar, to a fat-bottomed Cupid (saving your presence), who was kicking his heels in the air.—Ah! kick on, thought I; for the demon of traffic will ever fright away the loves and graces, that streak with the rosy beams of infant fancy the sombre day of life—whilst the imagination, not allowing us to see things as they are, enables us to catch a hasty draught of the running stream of delight, the thirst for which seems to be given only to tantalize us.

But I am philosophizing; nay, perhaps you will call me severe, and bid me let the square-headed money-getters alone.—Peace to them! though none of the social sprites (and there are not a few of different descriptions, who sport about the various inlets to my heart) gave me a twitch to restrain my pen.

I have been writing on, expecting poor — to come; for, when I began, I merely thought of business; and, as this is the idea that most naturally associates with your image, I wonder I stumbled on any other.

Yet, as common life, in my opinion, is scarcely worth having, even with a gigot every day, and a pudding added thereunto, I will allow you to cultivate my judgment, if you will permit me to keep alive the sentiments in your heart, which may be termed romantic, because, the offspring of the senses and the imagination, they resemble the mother more than the father,[7] when they produce the suffusion I admire.—In spite of icy age, I hope still to see it, if you have not determined only to eat and drink, and be stupidly useful to the stupid—

Yours,

MARY.

Havre, August 19 [1794] Tuesday.

I received both your letters to-day—I had reckoned on hearing from you yesterday, therefore was disappointed, though I imputed your silence to the right cause. I intended answering your kind letter immediately, that you might have felt the pleasure it gave me; but — came in, and some other things interrupted me; so that the fine vapour has evaporated—yet, leaving a sweet scent behind, I have only to tell you, what is sufficiently obvious, that the earnest desire I have shown to keep my place, or gain more ground in your heart, is a sure proof how necessary your affection is to my happiness.—Still I do not think it false delicacy, or foolish pride, to wish that your attention to my happiness should arise as much from love, which is always rather a selfish passion, as reason—that is, I want you to promote my felicity, by seeking your own.—For, whatever pleasure it may give me to discover your generosity of soul, I would not be dependent for your affection on the very quality I most admire. No; there are qualities in your heart, which demand my affection; but, unless the attachment appears to me clearly mutual, I shall labour only to esteem your character, instead of cherishing a tenderness for your person.

I write in a hurry, because the little one, who has been sleeping a long time, begins to call for me. Poor thing! when I am sad, I lament that all my affections grow on me, till they become too strong for my peace, though they all afford me snatches of exquisite enjoyment—This for our little girl was at first very reasonable—more the effect of reason, a sense of duty, than feeling—now, she has got into my heart and imagination, and when I walk out without her, her little figure is ever dancing before me.

You too have somehow clung round my heart—I found I could not eat my dinner in the great room—and, when I took up the large knife to carve for myself, tears rushed into my eyes.—Do not however suppose that I am melancholy—for, when you are from me, I not only wonder how I can find fault with you—but how I can doubt your affection.

I will not mix any comments on the inclosed (it roused my indignation) with the effusion of tenderness, with which I assure you, that you are the friend of my bosom, and the prop of my heart.

MARY.

Havre, August 20 [1794].

I want to know what steps you have taken respecting —. Knavery always rouses my indignation—I should be gratified to hear that the law had chastised — severely; but I do not wish you to see him, because the business does not now admit of peaceful discussion, and I do not exactly know how you would express your contempt.

Pray ask some questions about Tallien—I am still pleased with the dignity of his conduct.—The other day, in the cause of humanity, he made use of a degree of address, which I admire—and mean to point out to you, as one of the few instances of address which do credit to the abilities of the man, without taking away from that confidence in his openness of heart, which is the true basis of both public and private friendship.

Do not suppose that I mean to allude to a little reserve of temper in you, of which I have sometimes complained! You have been used to a cunning woman, and you almost look for cunning—Nay, in managing my happiness, you now and then wounded my sensibility, concealing yourself, till honest sympathy, giving you to me without disguise, lets me look into a heart, which my half-broken one wishes to creep into, to be revived and cherished.—You have frankness of heart, but not often exactly that overflowing (épanchement de coeur), which becoming almost childish, appears a weakness only to the weak.

But I have left poor Tallien. I wanted you to enquire likewise whether, as a member declared in the convention, Robespierre really maintained a number of mistresses.—Should it prove so, I suspect that they rather flattered his vanity than his senses.

Here is a chatting, desultory epistle! But do not suppose that I mean to close it without mentioning the little damsel—who has been almost springing out of my arm—she certainly looks very like you—but I do not love her the less for that, whether I am angry or pleased with you.

Yours affectionately,

MARY.

[Paris] September 22 [1794].

I have just written two letters, that are going by other conveyances, and which I reckon on your receiving long before this. I therefore merely write, because I know I should be disappointed at seeing any one who had left you, if you did not send a letter, were it ever so short, to tell me why you did not write a longer—and you will want to be told, over and over again, that our little Hercules is quite recovered.

Besides looking at me, there are three other things, which delight her—to ride in a coach, to look at a scarlet waistcoat, and hear loud music—yesterday, at the fête, she enjoyed the two latter; but, to honour J. J. Rousseau, I intend to give her a sash, the first she has ever had round her—and why not?—for I have always been half in love with him.

Well, this you will say is trifling—shall I talk about alum or soap? There is nothing picturesque in your present pursuits; my imagination then rather chuses to ramble back to the barrier with you, or to see you coming to meet me, and my basket of grapes.—With what pleasure do I recollect your looks and words, when I have been sitting on the window, regarding the waving corn!

Believe me, sage sir, you have not sufficient respect for the imagination—I could prove to you in a trice that it is the mother of sentiment, the great distinction of our nature, the only purifier of the passions—animals have a portion of reason, and equal, if not more exquisite, senses; but no trace of imagination, or her offspring taste, appears in any of their actions. The impulse of the senses, passions, if you will, and the conclusions of reason, draw men together; but the imagination is the true fire, stolen from heaven, to animate this cold creature of clay, producing all those fine sympathies that lead to rapture, rendering men social by expanding their hearts, instead of leaving them leisure to calculate how many comforts society affords.

If you call these observations romantic, a phrase in this place which would be tantamount to nonsensical, I shall be apt to retort, that you are embruted by trade, and the vulgar enjoyments of life—Bring me then back your barrier-face, or you shall have nothing to say to my barrier-girl; and I shall fly from you, to cherish the remembrances that will ever be dear to me; for I am yours truly,

MARY.

LETTER XXIV

[Paris] Evening, Sept. 23, [1794].

I have been playing and laughing with the little girl so long, that I cannot take up my pen to address you without emotion. Pressing her to my bosom, she looked so like you (entre nous, your best looks, for I do not admire your commercial face) every nerve seemed to vibrate to the touch, and I began to think that there was something in the assertion of man and wife being one—for you seemed to pervade my whole frame, quickening the beat of my heart, and lending me the sympathetic tears you excited.

Have I any thing more to say to you? No; not for the present—the rest is all flown away; and, indulging tenderness for you, I cannot now complain of some people here, who have ruffled my temper for two or three days past.

[Paris, 1794] Morning.

Yesterday B— sent to me for my packet of letters. He called on me before; and I like him better than I did—that is, I have the same opinion of his understanding, but I think with you, he has more tenderness and real delicacy of feeling with respect to women, than are commonly to be met with. His manner too of speaking of his little girl, about the age of mine, interested me. I gave him a letter for my sister, and requested him to see her.

I have been interrupted. Mr. — I suppose will write about business. Public affairs I do not descant on, except to tell you that they write now with great freedom and truth; and this liberty of the press will overthrow the Jacobins, I plainly perceive.

I hope you take care of your health. I have got a habit of restlessness at night, which arises, I believe, from activity of mind; for, when I am alone, that is, not near one to whom I can open my heart, I sink into reveries and trains of thinking, which agitate and fatigue me.

This is my third letter; when am I to hear from you? I need not tell you, I suppose, that I am now writing with somebody in the room with me, and — is waiting to carry this to Mr. —'s. I will then kiss the girl for you, and bid you adieu.

I desired you, in one of my other letters, to bring back to me your barrier-face—or that you should not be loved by my barrier-girl. I know that you will love her more and more, for she is a little affectionate, intelligent creature, with as much vivacity, I should think, as you could wish for.

I was going to tell you of two or three things which displease me here; but they are not of sufficient consequence to interrupt pleasing sensations. I have received a letter from Mr. —. I want you to bring — with you. Madame S— is by me, reading a German translation of your letters—she desires me to give her love to you, on account of what you say of the negroes.

Yours most affectionately,   MARY.

LETTER XXV

Paris, Sept. 28 [1794].

I have written to you three or four letters; but different causes have prevented my sending them by the persons who promised to take or forward them. The inclosed is one I wrote to go by B—; yet, finding that he will not arrive, before I hope, and believe, you will have set out on your return, I inclose it to you, and shall give it in charge to —, as Mr. — is detained, to whom I also gave a letter.

I cannot help being anxious to hear from you; but I shall not harrass you with accounts of inquietudes, or of cares that arise from peculiar circumstances.—I have had so many little plagues here, that I have almost lamented that I left Havre. —, who is at best a most helpless creature, is now, on account of her pregnancy, more trouble than use to me, so that I still continue to be almost a slave to the child.—She indeed rewards me, for she is a sweet little creature; for, setting aside a mother's fondness (which, by the bye, is growing on me, her little intelligent smiles sinking into my heart), she has an astonishing degree of sensibility and observation. The other day by B—'s child, a fine one, she looked like a little sprite.—She is all life and motion, and her eyes are not the eyes of a fool—I will swear.

I slept at St. Germain's, in the very room (if you have not forgot) in which you pressed me very tenderly to your heart.—I did not forget to fold my darling to mine, with sensations that are almost too sacred to be alluded to.

Adieu, my love! Take care of yourself, if you wish to be the protector of your child, and the comfort of her mother.

I have received, for you, letters from —. I want to hear how that affair finishes, though I do not know whether I have most contempt for his folly or knavery.

Your own

MARY.

[Paris] October 1 [1794].

It is a heartless task to write letters, without knowing whether they will ever reach you.—I have given two to —, who has been a-going, a-going, every day, for a week past; and three others, which were written in a low-spirited strain, a little querulous or so, I have not been able to forward by the opportunities that were mentioned to me. Tant mieux! you will say, and I will not say nay; for I should be sorry that the contents of a letter, when you are so far away, should damp the pleasure that the sight of it would afford—judging of your feelings by my own. I just now stumbled on one of the kind letters, which you wrote during your last absence. You are then a dear affectionate creature, and I will not plague you. The letter which you chance to receive, when the absence is so long, ought to bring only tears of tenderness, without any bitter alloy, into your eyes.

After your return I hope indeed, that you will not be so immersed in business, as during the last three or four months past—for even money, taking into the account all the future comforts it is to procure, may be gained at too dear a rate, if painful impressions are left on the mind.—These impressions were much more lively, soon after you went away, than at present—for a thousand tender recollections efface the melancholy traces they left on my mind—and every emotion is on the same side as my reason, which always was on yours.—Separated, it would be almost impious to dwell on real or imaginary imperfections of character.—I feel that I love you; and, if I cannot be happy with you, I will seek it no where else.

My little darling grows every day more dear to me—and she often has a kiss, when we are alone together, which I give her for you, with all my heart.

I have been interrupted—and must send off my letter. The liberty of the press will produce a great effect here—the cry of blood will not be vain!—Some more monsters will perish—and the Jacobins are conquered.—Yet I almost fear the last flap of the tail of the beast.

I have had several trifling teazing inconveniences here, which I shall not now trouble you with a detail of.—I am sending — back; her pregnancy rendered her useless. The girl I have got has more vivacity, which is better for the child.

I long to hear from you.—Bring a copy of — and — with you.

— is still here: he is a lost man.—He really loves his wife, and is anxious about his children; but his indiscriminate hospitality and social feelings have given him an inveterate habit of drinking, that destroys his health, as well as renders his person disgusting.—If his wife had more sense, or delicacy, she might restrain him: as it is, nothing will save him.

Yours most truly and affectionately

MARY.

[Paris] October 26 [1794].

My dear love, I began to wish so earnestly to hear from you, that the sight of your letters occasioned such pleasurable emotions, I was obliged to throw them aside till the little girl and I were alone together; and this said little girl, our darling, is become a most intelligent little creature, and as gay as a lark, and that in the morning too, which I do not find quite so convenient. I once told you, that the sensations before she was born, and when she is sucking, were pleasant; but they do not deserve to be compared to the emotions I feel, when she stops to smile upon me, or laughs outright on meeting me unexpectedly in the street, or after a short absence. She has now the advantage of having two good nurses, and I am at present able to discharge my duty to her, without being the slave of it.

I have therefore employed and amused myself since I got rid of —, and am making a progress in the language amongst other things. I have also made some new acquaintance. I have almost charmed a judge of the tribunal, R—, who, though I should not have thought it possible, has humanity, if not beaucoup d'esprit. But let me tell you, if you do not make haste back, I shall be half in love with the author of the Marseillaise, who is a handsome man, a little too broad-faced or so, and plays sweetly on the violin.

What do you say to this threat?—why, entre nous, I like to give way to a sprightly vein, when writing to you, that is, when I am pleased with you. "The devil," you know, is proverbially said to be "in a good humour, when he is pleased." Will you not then be a good boy, and come back quickly to play with your girls? but I shall not allow you to love the new-comer best.

My heart longs for your return, my love, and only looks for, and seeks happiness with you; yet do not imagine that I childishly wish you to come back, before you have arranged things in such a manner, that it will not be necessary for you to leave us soon again, or to make exertions which injure your constitution.

Yours most truly and tenderly,

MARY.

P.S. You would oblige me by delivering the inclosed to Mr. —, and pray call for an answer.—It is for a person uncomfortably situated.

[Paris] Dec. 26 [1794].

I have been, my love, for some days tormented by fears, that I would not allow to assume a form—I had been expecting you daily—and I heard that many vessels had been driven on shore during the late gale.—Well, I now see your letter—and find that you are safe; I will not regret then that your exertions have hitherto been so unavailing.

Be that as it may, return to me when you have arranged the other matters, which — has been crowding on you. I want to be sure that you are safe—and not separated from me by a sea that must be passed. For, feeling that I am happier than I ever was, do you wonder at my sometimes dreading that fate has not done persecuting me? Come to me, my dearest friend, husband, father of my child!—All these fond ties glow at my heart at this moment, and dim my eyes.—With you an independence is desirable; and it is always within our reach, if affluence escapes us—without you the world again appears empty to me. But I am recurring to some of the melancholy thoughts that have flitted across my mind for some days past, and haunted my dreams.

My little darling is indeed a sweet child; and I am sorry that you are not here, to see her little mind unfold itself. You talk of "dalliance;" but certainly no lover was ever more attached to his mistress, than she is to me. Her eyes follow me every where, and by affection I have the most despotic power over her. She is all vivacity or softness—yes; I love her more than I thought I should. When I have been hurt at your stay, I have embraced her as my only comfort—when pleased with you, for looking and laughing like you; nay, I cannot, I find, long be angry with you, whilst I am kissing her for resembling you. But there would be no end to these details. Fold us both to your heart; for I am truly and affectionately

Yours,

MARY.

[Paris] December 28 [1794].

I do, my love, indeed sincerely sympathize with you in all your disappointments.—Yet, knowing that you are well, and think of me with affection, I only lament other disappointments, because I am sorry that you should thus exert yourself in vain, and that you are kept from me.

—, I know, urges you to stay, and is continually branching out into new projects, because he has the idle desire to amass a large fortune, rather an immense one, merely to have the credit of having made it. But we who are governed by other motives, ought not to be led on by him. When we meet, we will discuss this subject—You will listen to reason, and it has probably occurred to you, that it will be better, in future, to pursue some sober plan, which may demand more time, and still enable you to arrive at the same end. It appears to me absurd to waste life in preparing to live.

Would it not now be possible to arrange your business in such a manner as to avoid the inquietudes, of which I have had my share since your departure? Is it not possible to enter into business, as an employment necessary to keep the faculties awake, and (to sink a little in the expressions) the pot boiling, without suffering what must ever be considered as a secondary object, to engross the mind, and drive sentiment and affection out of the heart?

I am in a hurry to give this letter to the person who has promised to forward it with —'s. I wish then to counteract, in some measure, what he has doubtless recommended most warmly.

Stay, my friend, whilst it is absolutely necessary.—I will give you no tenderer name, though it glows at my heart, unless you come the moment the settling the present objects permit.—I do not consent to your taking any other journey—or the little woman and I will be off, the Lord knows where. But, as I had rather owe every thing to your affection, and, I may add, to your reason, (for this immoderate desire of wealth, which makes — so eager to have you remain, is contrary to your principles of action), I will not importune you.—I will only tell you, that I long to see you—and, being at peace with you, I shall be hurt, rather than made angry, by delays.—Having suffered so much in life, do not be surprised if I sometimes, when left to myself, grow gloomy, and suppose that it was all a dream, and that my happiness is not to last. I say happiness, because remembrance retrenches all the dark shades of the picture.

My little one begins to show her teeth, and use her legs—She wants you to bear your part in the nursing business, for I am fatigued with dancing her, and yet she is not satisfied—she wants you to thank her mother for taking such care of her, as you only can.

Yours truly,

MARY.

LETTER XXX

[Paris] December 29 [1794].

Though I suppose you have later intelligence, yet, as — has just informed me that he has an opportunity of sending immediately to you, I take advantage of it to inclose you

How I hate this crooked business! This intercourse with the world, which obliges one to see the worst side of human nature! Why cannot you be content with the object you had first in view, when you entered into this wearisome labyrinth?—I know very well that you have imperceptibly been drawn on; yet why does one project, successful or abortive, only give place to two others? Is it not sufficient to avoid poverty?—I am contented to do my part; and, even here, sufficient to escape from wretchedness is not difficult to obtain. And, let me tell you, I have my project also—and, if you do not soon return, the little girl and I will take care of ourselves; we will not accept any of your cold kindness—your distant civilities—no; not we.

This is but half jesting, for I am really tormented by the desire which — manifests to have you remain where you are.—Yet why do I talk to you?—If he can persuade you—let him!—for, if you are not happier with me, and your own wishes do not make you throw aside these eternal projects, I am above using any arguments, though reason as well as affection seems to offer them—if our affection be mutual, they will occur to you—and you will act accordingly.

Since my arrival here, I have found the German lady, of whom you have heard me speak. Her first child died in the month; but she has another, about the age of my Fanny, a fine little creature. They are still but contriving to live—earning their daily bread—yet, though they are but just above poverty, I envy them.—She is a tender, affectionate mother—fatigued even by her attention.—However she has an affectionate husband in her turn, to render her care light, and to share her pleasure.

I will own to you that, feeling extreme tenderness for my little girl, I grow sad very often when I am playing with her, that you are not here, to observe with me how her mind unfolds, and her little heart becomes attached!—These appear to me to be true pleasures—and still you suffer them to escape you, in search of what we may never enjoy.—It is your own maxim to "live in the present moment."—If you do—stay, for God's sake; but tell me the truth—if not, tell me when I may expect to see you, and let me not be always vainly looking for you, till I grow sick at heart.

Adieu! I am a little hurt.—I must take my darling to my bosom to comfort me.

MARY.

LETTER XXXI

[Paris] December 30 [1794].

Should you receive three or four of the letters at once which I have written lately, do not think of Sir John Brute, for I do not mean to wife you. I only take advantage of every occasion, that one out of three of my epistles may reach your hands, and inform you that I am not of —'s opinion, who talks till he makes me angry, of the necessity of your staying two or three months longer. I do not like this life of continual inquietude—and, entre nous, I am determined to try to earn some money here myself, in order to convince you that, if you chuse to run about the world to get a fortune, it is for yourself—for the little girl and I will live without your assistance, unless you are with us. I may be termed proud—Be it so—but I will never abandon certain principles of action.

The common run of men have such an ignoble way of thinking, that, if they debauch their hearts, and prostitute their persons, following perhaps a gust of inebriation, they suppose the wife, slave rather, whom they maintain, has no right to complain, and ought to receive the sultan, whenever he deigns to return, with open arms, though his have been polluted by half an hundred promiscuous amours during his absence.

I consider fidelity and constancy as two distinct things; yet the former is necessary, to give life to the other—and such a degree of respect do I think due to myself, that, if only probity, which is a good thing in its place, brings you back, never return!—for, if a wandering of the heart, or even a caprice of the imagination detains you—there is an end of all my hopes of happiness—I could not forgive it, if I would.

I have gotten into a melancholy mood, you perceive. You know my opinion of men in general; you know that I think them systematic tyrants, and that it is the rarest thing in the world, to meet with a man with sufficient delicacy of feeling to govern desire. When I am thus sad, I lament that my little darling, fondly as I doat on her, is a girl.—I am sorry to have a tie to a world that for me is ever sown with thorns.

You will call this an ill-humoured letter, when, in fact, it is the strongest proof of affection I can give, to dread to lose you. — has taken such pains to convince me that you must and ought to stay, that it has inconceivably depressed my spirits—You have always known my opinion—I have ever declared, that two people, who mean to live together, ought not to be long separated.—If certain things are more necessary to you than me—search for them—Say but one word, and you shall never hear of me more.— If not—for God's sake, let us struggle with poverty—with any evil, but these continual inquietudes of business, which I have been told were to last but a few months, though every day the end appears more distant! This is the first letter in this strain that I have determined to forward to you; the rest lie by, because I was unwilling to give you pain, and I should not now write, if I did not think that there would be no conclusion to the schemes, which demand, as I am told, your presence.

MARY.[9]

[Paris] January 9 [1795].

I just now received one of your hasty notes; for business so entirely occupies you, that you have not time, or sufficient command of thought, to write letters. Beware! you seem to be got into a whirl of projects and schemes, which are drawing you into a gulph, that, if it do not absorb your happiness, will infallibly destroy mine.

Fatigued during my youth by the most arduous struggles, not only to obtain independence, but to render myself useful, not merely pleasure, for which I had the most lively taste, I mean the simple pleasures that flow from passion and affection, escaped me, but the most melancholy views of life were impressed by a disappointed heart on my mind. Since I knew you, I have been endeavouring to go back to my former nature, and have allowed some time to glide away, winged with the delight which only spontaneous enjoyment can give.—Why have you so soon dissolved the charm.

I am really unable to bear the continual inquietude which your and —'s never-ending plans produce. This you may term want of firmness—but you are mistaken—I have still sufficient firmness to pursue my principle of action. The present misery, I cannot find a softer word to do justice to my feelings, appears to me unnecessary—and therefore I have not firmness to support it as you may think I ought. I should have been content, and still wish, to retire with you to a farm—My God! any thing, but these continual anxieties—any thing but commerce, which debases the mind, and roots out affection from the heart.

I do not mean to complain of subordinate inconveniences—yet I will simply observe, that, led to expect you every week, I did not make the arrangements required by the present circumstances, to procure the necessaries of life. In order to have them, a servant, for that purpose only, is indispensible—The want of wood, has made me catch the most violent cold I ever had; and my head is so disturbed by continual coughing, that I am unable to write without stopping frequently to recollect myself.—This however is one of the common evils which must be borne with—bodily pain does not touch the heart, though it fatigues the spirits.

Still as you talk of your return, even in February, doubtingly, I have determined, the moment the weather changes, to wean my child.—It is too soon for her to begin to divide sorrow!—And as one has well said, "despair is a freeman," we will go and seek our fortune together.

This is not a caprice of the moment—for your absence has given new weight to some conclusions, that I was very reluctantly forming before you left me.—I do not chuse to be a secondary object.—If your feelings were in unison with mine, you would not sacrifice so much to visionary prospects of future advantage.

MARY.

LETTER XXXIII

[Paris] Jan. 15 [1795].

I was just going to begin my letter with the fag end of a song, which would only have told you, what I may as well say simply, that it is pleasant to forgive those we love. I have received your two letters, dated the 26th and 28th of December, and my anger died away. You can scarcely conceive the effect some of your letters have produced on me. After longing to hear from you during a tedious interval of suspense, I have seen a superscription written by you.—Promising myself pleasure, and feeling emotion, I have laid it by me, till the person who brought it, left the room—when, behold! on opening it, I have found only half a dozen hasty lines, that have damped all the rising affection of my soul.

Well, now for business—

My animal is well; I have not yet taught her to eat, but nature is doing the business. I gave her a crust to assist the cutting of her teeth; and now she has two, she makes good use of them to gnaw a crust, biscuit, &c. You would laugh to see her; she is just like a little squirrel; she will guard a crust for two hours; and, after fixing her eye on an object for some time, dart on it with an aim as sure as a bird of prey—nothing can equal her life and spirits. I suffer from a cold; but it does not affect her. Adieu! do not forget to love us—and come soon to tell us that you do.

MARY.

LETTER XXXIV

[Paris] Jan. 30 [1795].

From the purport of your last letters, I should suppose that this will scarcely reach you; and I have already written so many letters, that you have either not received, or neglected to acknowledge, I do not find it pleasant, or rather I have no inclination, to go over the same ground again. If you have received them, and are still detained by new projects, it is useless for me to say any more on the subject. I have done with it for ever; yet I ought to remind you that your pecuniary interest suffers by your absence.

For my part, my head is turned giddy, by only hearing of plans to make money, and my contemptuous feelings have sometimes burst out. I therefore was glad that a violent cold gave me a pretext to stay at home, lest I should have uttered unseasonable truths.

My child is well, and the spring will perhaps restore me to myself.—I have endured many inconveniences this winter, which should I be ashamed to mention, if they had been unavoidable. "The secondary pleasures of life," you say, "are very necessary to my comfort:" it may be so; but I have ever considered them as secondary. If therefore you accuse me of wanting the resolution necessary to bear the common[10] evils of life; I should answer, that I have not fashioned my mind to sustain them, because I would avoid them, cost what it would—

Adieu!

MARY.

LETTER XXXV

[Paris] February 9 [1795].

The melancholy presentiment has for some time hung on my spirits, that we were parted for ever; and the letters I received this day, by Mr. —, convince me that it was not without foundation. You allude to some other letters, which I suppose have miscarried; for most of those I have got, were only a few hasty lines, calculated to wound the tenderness the sight of the superscriptions excited.

I mean not however to complain; yet so many feelings are struggling for utterance, and agitating a heart almost bursting with anguish, that I find it very difficult to write with any degree of coherence.

You left me indisposed, though you have taken no notice of it; and the most fatiguing journey I ever had, contributed to continue it. However, I recovered my health; but a neglected cold, and continual inquietude during the last two months, have reduced me to a state of weakness I never before experienced. Those who did not know that the canker-worm was at work at the core, cautioned me about suckling my child too long.—God preserve this poor child, and render her happier than her mother!

But I am wandering from my subject: indeed my head turns giddy, when I think that all the confidence I have had in the affection of others is come to this.—I did not expect this blow from you. I have done my duty to you and my child; and if I am not to have any return of affection to reward me, I have the sad consolation of knowing that I deserved a better fate. My soul is weary—I am sick at heart; and, but for this little darling, I would cease to care about a life, which is now stripped of every charm.

You see how stupid I am, uttering declamation, when I meant simply to tell you, that I consider your requesting me to come to you, as merely dictated by honour.—Indeed, I scarcely understand you.—You request me to come, and then tell me, that you have not given up all thoughts of returning to this place.

When I determined to live with you, I was only governed by affection.—I would share poverty with you, but I turn with affright from the sea of trouble on which you are entering.—I have certain principles of action: I know what I look for to found my happiness on.—It is not money.—With you I wished for sufficient to procure the comforts of life—as it is, less will do.—I can still exert myself to obtain the necessaries of life for my child, and she does not want more at present.—I have two or three plans in my head to earn our subsistence; for do not suppose that, neglected by you, I will lie under obligations of a pecuniary kind to you!—No; I would sooner submit to menial service.—I wanted the support of your affection—that gone, all is over!—I did not think, when I complained of —'s contemptible avidity to accumulate money, that he would have dragged you into his schemes.

I cannot write.—I inclose a fragment of a letter, written soon after your departure, and another which tenderness made me keep back when it was written.—You will see then the sentiments of a calmer, though not a more determined, moment.—Do not insult me by saying, that "our being together is paramount to every other consideration!" Were it, you would not be running after a bubble, at the expence of my peace of mind.

Perhaps this is the last letter you will ever receive from me.

MARY.

LETTER XXXVI

[Paris] Feb. 10 [1795].

You talk of "permanent views and future comfort"—not for me, for I am dead to hope. The inquietudes of the last winter have finished the business, and my heart is not only broken, but my constitution destroyed. I conceive myself in a galloping consumption, and the continual anxiety I feel at the thought of leaving my child, feeds the fever that nightly devours me. It is on her account that I again write to you, to conjure you, by all that you hold sacred, to leave her here with the German lady you may have heard me mention! She has a child of the same age, and they may be brought up together, as I wish her to be brought up. I shall write more fully on the subject. To facilitate this, I shall give up my present lodgings, and go into the same house. I can live much cheaper there, which is now become an object. I have had 3000 livres from —, and I shall take one more, to pay my servant's wages, &c. and then I shall endeavour to procure what I want by my own exertions. I shall entirely give up the acquaintance of the Americans.

— and I have not been on good terms a long time. Yesterday he very unmanlily exulted over me, on account of your determination to stay. I had provoked it, it is true, by some asperities against commerce, which have dropped from me, when we have argued about the propriety of your remaining where you are; and it is no matter, I have drunk too deep of the bitter cup to care about trifles.

When you first entered into these plans, you bounded your views to the gaining of a thousand pounds. It was sufficient to have procured a farm in America, which would have been an independence. You find now that you did not know yourself, and that a certain situation in life is more necessary to you than you imagined—more necessary than an uncorrupted heart—For a year or two, you may procure yourself what you call pleasure; eating, drinking, and women; but in the solitude of declining life, I shall be remembered with regret—I was going to say with remorse, but checked my pen.

As I have never concealed the nature of my connection with you, your reputation will not suffer. I shall never have a confident: I am content with the approbation of my own mind; and, if there be a searcher of hearts, mine will not be despised. Reading what you have written relative to the desertion of women, I have often wondered how theory and practice could be so different, till I recollected, that the sentiments of passion, and the resolves of reason, are very distinct. As to my sisters, as you are so continually hurried with business, you need not write to them—I shall, when my mind is calmer. God bless you! Adieu!

MARY.

This has been such a period of barbarity and misery, I ought not to complain of having my share. I wish one moment that I had never heard of the cruelties that have been practised here, and the next envy the mothers who have been killed with their children. Surely I had suffered enough in life, not to be cursed with a fondness, that burns up the vital stream I am imparting. You will think me mad: I would I were so, that I could forget my misery—so that my head or heart would be still.—

LETTER XXXVII

[Paris] Feb. 19 [1795].

When I first received your letter, putting off your return to an indefinite time, I felt so hurt, that I know not what I wrote. I am now calmer, though it was not the kind of wound over which time has the quickest effect; on the contrary, the more I think, the sadder I grow. Society fatigues me inexpressibly— So much so, that finding fault with every one, I have only reason enough, to discover that the fault is in myself. My child alone interests me, and, but for her, I should not take any pains to recover my health.

As it is, I shall wean her, and try if by that step (to which I feel a repugnance, for it is my only solace) I can get rid of my cough. Physicians talk much of the danger attending any complaint on the lungs, after a woman has suckled for some months. They lay a stress also on the necessity of keeping the mind tranquil—and, my God! how has mine be harrassed! But whilst the caprices of other women are gratified, "the wind of heaven not suffered to visit them too rudely," I have not found a guardian angel, in heaven or on earth, to ward off sorrow or care from my bosom.

What sacrifices have you not made for a woman you did not respect!—But I will not go over this ground—I want to tell you that I do not understand you. You say that you have not given up all thoughts of returning here—and I know that it will be necessary—nay, is. I cannot explain myself; but if you have not lost your memory, you will easily divine my meaning. What! is our life then only to be made up of separations? and am I only to return to a country, that has not merely lost all charms for me, but for which I feel a repugnance that almost amounts to horror, only to be left there a prey to it!

Why is it so necessary that I should return?—brought up here, my girl would be freer. Indeed, expecting you to join us, I had formed some plans of usefulness that have now vanished with my hopes of happiness.

In the bitterness of my heart, I could complain with reason, that I am left here dependent on a man, whose avidity to acquire a fortune has rendered him callous to every sentiment connected with social or affectionate emotions.—With a brutal insensibility, he cannot help displaying the pleasure your determination to stay gives him, in spite of the effect it is visible it has had on me.

Till I can earn money, I shall endeavour to borrow some, for I want to avoid asking him continually for the sum necessary to maintain me.—Do not mistake me, I have never been refused.—Yet I have gone half a dozen times to the house to ask for it, and come away without speaking—you must guess why—Besides, I wish to avoid hearing of the eternal projects to which you have sacrificed my peace—not remembering—but I will be silent for ever.—

LETTER XXXVIII

[Havre] April 7 [1795].

Here I am at Havre, on the wing towards you, and I write now, only to tell you, that you may expect me in the course of three or four days; for I shall not attempt to give vent to the different emotions which agitate my heart—You may term a feeling, which appears to me to be a degree of delicacy that naturally arises from sensibility, pride—Still I cannot indulge the very affectionate tenderness which glows in my bosom, without trembling, till I see, by your eyes, that it is mutual.

I sit, lost in thought, looking at the sea—and tears rush into my eyes, when I find that I am cherishing any fond expectations.—I have indeed been so unhappy this winter, I find it as difficult to acquire fresh hopes, as to regain tranquillity.—Enough of this—lie still, foolish heart!—But for the little girl, I could almost wish that it should cease to beat, to be no more alive to the anguish of disappointment.

Sweet little creature! I deprived myself of my only pleasure, when I weaned her, about ten days ago.—I am however glad I conquered my repugnance.—It was necessary it should be done soon, and I did not wish to embitter the renewal of your acquaintance with her, by putting it off till we met.—It was a painful exertion to me, and I thought it best to throw this inquietude with the rest, into the sack that I would fain throw over my shoulder.—I wished to endure it alone, in short—Yet, after sending her to sleep in the next room for three or four nights, you cannot think with what joy I took her back again to sleep in my bosom!

I suppose I shall find you, when I arrive, for I do not see any necessity for your coming to me.—Pray inform Mr. —, that I have his little friend with me.—My wishing to oblige him, made me put myself to some inconvenience—and delay my departure; which was irksome to me, who have not quite as much philosophy, I would not for the world say indifference, as you. God bless you!

Yours truly

MARY.

Brighthelmstone, Saturday, April 11 [1795].

Here we are, my love, and mean to set out early in the morning; and, if I can find you, I hope to dine with you to-morrow.—I shall drive to —'s hotel, where — tells me you have been—and, if you have left it, I hope you will take care to be there to receive us.

I have brought with me Mr. —'s little friend, and a girl whom I like to take care of our little darling—not on the way, for that fell to my share.—But why do I write about trifles?—or any thing?—Are we not to meet soon?—What does your heart say?

Yours truly

MARY.

I have weaned my Fanny, and she is now eating away at the white bread.

[26 Charlotte Street, Rathbone Place] London, Friday, May 22 [1795].

I have just received your affectionate letter, and am distressed to think that I have added to your embarrassments at this troublesome juncture, when the exertion of all the faculties of your mind appears to be necessary, to extricate you out of your pecuniary difficulties. I suppose it was something relative to the circumstance you have mentioned, which made — request to see me to-day, to converse about a matter of great importance. Be that as it may, his letter (such is the state of my spirits) inconceivably alarmed me, and rendered the last night as distressing, as the two former had been.

I have laboured to calm my mind since you left me—Still I find that tranquillity is not to be obtained by exertion; it is a feeling so different from the resignation of despair!—I am however no longer angry with you—nor will I ever utter another complaint—there are arguments which convince the reason, whilst they carry death to the heart.—We have had too many cruel explanations, that not only cloud every future prospect; but embitter the remembrances which alone give life to affection.—Let the subject never be revived!

It seems to me that I have not only lost the hope, but the power of being happy.—Every emotion is now sharpened by anguish.—My soul has been shook, and my tone of feelings destroyed.—I have gone out—and sought for dissipation, if not amusement, merely to fatigue still more, I find, my irritable nerves—

My friend—my dear friend—examine yourself well—I am out of the question; for, alas! I am nothing—and discover what you wish to do—what will render you most comfortable—or, to be more explicit—

whether you desire to live with me, or part for ever? When you can once ascertain it, tell me frankly, I conjure you!—for, believe me, I have very involuntarily interrupted your peace.

I shall expect you to dinner on Monday, and will endeavour to assume a cheerful face to greet you—at any rate I will avoid conversations, which only tend to harrass your feelings, because I am most affectionately yours,

MARY.

[May 27, 1795] Wednesday.

I inclose you the letter, which you desired me to forward, and I am tempted very laconically to wish you a good morning—not because I am angry, or have nothing to say; but to keep down a wounded spirit.—I shall make every effort to calm my mind—yet a strong conviction seems to whirl round in the very centre of my brain, which, like the fiat of fate, emphatically assures me, that grief has a firm hold of my heart.

God bless you!

Yours sincerely,

MARY.

[Hull] Wednesday, Two o'Clock [May 27, 1795].

We arrived here about an hour ago. I am extremely fatigued with the child, who would not rest quiet with any body but me, during the night—and now we are here in a comfortless, damp room, in a sort of a tomb-like house. This however I shall quickly remedy, for, when I have finished this letter, (which I must do immediately, because the post goes out early), I shall sally forth, and enquire about a vessel and an inn.

I will not distress you by talking of the depression of my spirits, or the struggle I had to keep alive my dying heart.—It is even now too full to allow me to write with composure.—Imlay,—dear Imlay,—am I always to be tossed about thus?—shall I never find an asylum to rest contented in? How can you love to fly about continually—dropping down, as it were, in a new world—cold and strange!—every other day? Why do you not attach those tender emotions round the idea of home, which even now dim my eyes?—This alone is affection—every thing else is only humanity, electrified by sympathy.

I will write to you again to-morrow, when I know how long I am to be detained—and hope to get a letter quickly from you, to cheer yours sincerely and affectionately

MARY.

Fanny is playing near me in high spirits. She was so pleased with the noise of the mail-horn, she has been continually imitating it.—Adieu!

[Hull, May 28, 1795] Thursday.

A lady has just sent to offer to take me to Beverley. I have then only a moment to exclaim against the vague manner in which people give information

But why talk of inconveniences, which are in fact trifling, when compared with the sinking of the heart I have felt! I did not intend to touch this painful string—God bless you!

Yours truly,

MARY.

[Hull] Friday, June 12 [1795].

I have just received yours dated the 9th, which I suppose was a mistake, for it could scarcely have loitered so long on the road. The general observations which apply to the state of your own mind, appear to me just, as far as they go; and I shall always consider it as one of the most serious misfortunes of my life, that I did not meet you, before satiety had rendered your senses so fastidious, as almost to close up every tender avenue of sentiment and affection that leads to your sympathetic heart. You have a heart, my friend, yet, hurried away by the impetuosity of inferior feelings, you have sought in vulgar excesses, for that gratification which only the heart can bestow.

The common run of men, I know, with strong health and gross appetites, must have variety to banish ennui, because the imagination never lends its magic wand, to convert appetite into love, cemented by according reason.—Ah! my friend, you know not the ineffable delight, the exquisite pleasure, which arises from a unison of affection and desire, when the whole soul and senses are abandoned to a lively imagination, that renders every emotion delicate and rapturous. Yes; these are emotions, over which satiety has no power, and the recollection of which, even disappointment cannot disenchant; but they do not exist without self-denial. These emotions, more or less strong, appear to me to be the distinctive characteristic of genius, the foundation of taste, and of that exquisite relish for the beauties of nature, of which the common herd of eaters and drinkers and child-begeters, certainly have no idea. You will smile at an observation that has just occurred to me:—I consider those minds as the most strong and original, whose imagination acts as the stimulus to their senses.

Well! you will ask, what is the result of all this reasoning? Why I cannot help thinking that it is possible for you, having great strength of mind, to return to nature, and regain a sanity of constitution, and purity of feeling—which would open your heart to me.—I would fain rest there!

Yet, convinced more than ever of the sincerity and tenderness of my attachment to you, the involuntary hopes, which a determination to live has revived, are not sufficiently strong to dissipate the cloud, that despair has spread over futurity. I have looked at the sea, and at my child, hardly daring to own to myself the secret wish, that it might become our tomb; and that the heart, still so alive to anguish, might there be quieted by death. At this moment ten thousand complicated sentiments press for utterance, weigh on my heart, and obscure my sight.

Are we ever to meet again? and will you endeavour to render that meeting happier than the last? Will you endeavour to restrain your caprices, in order to give vigour to affection, and to give play to the checked sentiments that nature intended should expand your heart? I cannot indeed, without agony, think of your bosom's being continually contaminated; and bitter are the tears which exhaust my eyes, when I recollect why my child and I are forced to stray from the asylum, in which, after so many storms, I had hoped to rest, smiling at angry fate.—These are not common sorrows; nor can you perhaps conceive, how much active fortitude it requires to labour perpetually to blunt the shafts of disappointment.

Examine now yourself, and ascertain whether you can live in something like a settled stile. Let our confidence in future be unbounded; consider whether you find it necessary to sacrifice me to what you term "the zest of life;" and, when you have once a clear view of your own motives, of your own incentive to action, do not deceive me!

The train of thoughts which the writing of this epistle awoke, makes me so wretched, that I must take a walk, to rouse and calm my mind. But first, let me tell you, that, if you really wish to promote my happiness, you will endeavour to give me as much as you can of yourself. You have great mental energy; and your judgment seems to me so just, that it is only the dupe of your inclination in discussing one subject.

The post does not go out to-day. To-morrow I may write more tranquilly. I cannot yet say when the vessel will sail in which I have determined to depart.

[Hull, June 13, 1795] Saturday Morning.

Your second letter reached me about an hour ago. You were certainly wrong, in supposing that I did not mention you with respect; though, without my being conscious of it, some sparks of resentment may have animated the gloom of despair—Yes; with less affection, I should have been more respectful. However the regard which I have for you, is so unequivocal to myself, I imagine that it must be sufficiently obvious to every body else. Besides, the only letter I intended for the public eye was to —, and that I destroyed from delicacy before you saw them, because it was only written (of course warmly in your praise) to prevent any odium being thrown on you.[11]

I am harrassed by your embarrassments, and shall certainly use all my efforts, to make the business terminate to your satisfaction in which I am engaged.

My friend—my dearest friend—I feel my fate united to yours by the most sacred principles of my soul, and the yearns of—yes, I will say it—a true, unsophisticated heart.

Yours most truly

MARY.

If the wind be fair, the captain talks of sailing on Monday; but I am afraid I shall be detained some days longer. At any rate, continue to write, (I want this support) till you are sure I am where I cannot expect a letter; and, if any should arrive after my departure, a gentleman (not Mr. —'s friend, I promise you) from whom I have received great civilities, will send them after me.

Do write by every occasion! I am anxious to hear how your affairs go on; and, still more, to be convinced that you are not separating yourself from us. For my little darling is calling papa, and adding her parrot word—Come, Come! And will you not come, and let us exert ourselves?—I shall recover all my energy, when I am convinced that my exertions will draw us more closely together. Once more adieu!

LETTER XLV

[Hull] Sunday, June 14 [1795].

I rather expected to hear from you to-day—I wish you would not fail to write to me for a little time, because I am not quite well—Whether I have any good sleep or not, I wake in the morning in violent fits of trembling—and, in spite of all my efforts, the child—every thing—fatigues me, in which I seek for solace or amusement.

Mr. — forced on me a letter to a physician of this place; it was fortunate, for I should otherwise have had some difficulty to obtain the necessary information. His wife is a pretty woman (I can admire, you know, a pretty woman, when I am alone) and he an intelligent and rather interesting man.—They have behaved to me with great hospitality; and poor Fanny was never so happy in her life, as amongst their young brood.

They took me in their carriage to Beverley, and I ran over my favourite walks, with a vivacity that would have astonished you.—The town did not please me quite so well as formerly—It appeared so diminutive; and, when I found that many of the inhabitants had lived in the same houses ever since I left it, I could not help wondering how they could thus have vegetated, whilst I was running over a world of sorrow, snatching at pleasure, and throwing off prejudices. The place where I at present am, is much improved; but it is astonishing what strides aristocracy and fanaticism have made, since I resided in this country.

The wind does not appear inclined to change, so I am still forced to linger—When do you think that you shall be able to set out for France? I do not entirely like the aspect of your affairs, and still less your connections on either side of the water. Often do I sigh, when I think of your entanglements in business, and your extreme restlessness of mind.—Even now I am almost afraid to ask you, whether the pleasure of being free, does not overbalance the pain you felt at parting with me? Sometimes I indulge the hope that you will feel me necessary to you—or why should we meet again?—but, the moment after, despair damps my rising spirits, aggravated by the emotions of tenderness, which ought to soften the cares of life.—God bless you!

Yours sincerely and affectionately

MARY.

LETTER XLVI

[Hull] June 15 [1795].

I want to know how you have settled with respect to —. In short, be very particular in your account of all your affairs—let our confidence, my dear, be unbounded.—The last time we were separated, was a separation indeed on your part—Now you have acted more ingenuously, let the most affectionate interchange of sentiments fill up the aching void of disappointment. I almost dread that your plans will prove abortive—yet should the most unlucky turn send you home to us, convinced that a true friend is a treasure, I should not much mind having to struggle with the world again. Accuse me not of pride—yet sometimes, when nature has opened my heart to its author, I have wondered that you did not set a higher value on my heart.

Receive a kiss from Fanny, I was going to add, if you will not take one from me, and believe me yours

Sincerely

MARY.

The wind still continues in the same quarter.

LETTER XLVII

[Hull, June, 1795] Tuesday Morning.

The captain has just sent to inform me, that I must be on board in the course of a few hours.—I wished to have stayed till to-morrow. It would have been a comfort to me to have received another letter from you—Should one arrive, it will be sent after me.

My spirits are agitated, I scarcely know why—The quitting England seems to be a fresh parting.—Surely you will not forget me.—A thousand weak forebodings assault my soul, and the state of my health renders me sensible to every thing. It is surprising that in London, in a continual conflict of mind, I was still growing better—whilst here, bowed down by the despotic hand of fate, forced into resignation by despair, I seem to be fading away—perishing beneath a cruel blight, that withers up all my faculties.

The child is perfectly well. My hand seems unwilling to add adieu! I know not why this inexpressible sadness has taken possession of me.—It is not a presentiment of ill. Yet, having been so perpetually the sport of disappointment,—having a heart that has been as it were a mark for misery, I dread to meet wretchedness in some new shape.—Well, let it come—I care not!—what have I to dread, who have so little to hope for! God bless you—I am most affectionately and sincerely yours

MARY.

LETTER XLVIII

[June 17, 1795] Wednesday Morning.

I was hurried on board yesterday about three o'clock, the wind having changed. But before evening it veered round to the old point; and here we are, in the midst of mists and water, only taking advantage of the tide to advance a few miles.

You will scarcely suppose that I left the town with reluctance—yet it was even so—for I wished to receive another letter from you, and I felt pain at parting, for ever perhaps, from the amiable family, who had treated me with so much hospitality and kindness. They will probably send me your letter, if it arrives this morning; for here we are likely to remain, I am afraid to think how long.

The vessel is very commodious, and the captain a civil, open-hearted kind of man. There being no other passengers, I have the cabin to myself, which is pleasant; and I have brought a few books with me to beguile weariness; but I seem inclined, rather to employ the dead moments of suspence in writing some effusions, than in reading.

What are you about? How are your affairs going on? It may be a long time before you answer these questions. My dear friend, my heart sinks within me!—Why am I forced thus to struggle continually with my affections and feelings?—Ah! why are those affections and feelings the source of so much misery, when they seem to have been given to vivify my heart, and extend my usefulness! But I must not dwell on this subject.—Will you not endeavour to cherish all the affection you can for me? What am I saying?—Rather forget me, if you can—if other gratifications are dearer to you.—How is every remembrance of mine embittered by disappointment? What a world is this!—They only seem happy, who never look beyond sensual or artificial enjoyments.—Adieu!

Fanny begins to play with the cabin-boy, and is as gay as a lark.—I will labour to be tranquil; and am in every mood,

Yours sincerely

MARY.

LETTER XLIX

[June 18, 1795] Thursday.

Here I am still—and I have just received your letter of Monday by the pilot, who promised to bring it to me, if we were detained, as he expected, by the wind.—It is indeed wearisome to be thus tossed about without going forward.—I have a violent headache—yet I am obliged to take care of the child, who is a little tormented by her teeth, because — is unable to do any thing, she is rendered so sick by the motion of the ship, as we ride at anchor.

These are however trifling inconveniences, compared with anguish of mind—compared with the sinking of a broken heart.—To tell you the truth, I never suffered in my life so much from depression of spirits—from despair.—I do not sleep—or, if I close my eyes, it is to have the most terrifying dreams, in which I often meet you with different casts of countenance.

I will not, my dear Imlay, torment you by dwelling on my sufferings—and will use all my efforts to calm my mind, instead of deadening it—at present it is most painfully active. I find I am not equal to these continual struggles—yet your letter this morning has afforded me some comfort—and I will try to revive hope. One thing let me tell you—when we meet again—surely we are to meet!—it must be to part no more. I mean not to have seas between us—it is more than I can support.

The pilot is hurrying me—God bless you.

In spite of the commodiousness of the vessel, every thing here would disgust my senses, had I nothing else to think of—"When the mind's free, the body's delicate;"—mine has been too much hurt to regard trifles.

Yours most truly

MARY.

LETTER L

[June 20, 1795] Saturday.

This is the fifth dreary day I have been imprisoned by the wind, with every outward object to disgust the senses, and unable to banish the remembrances that sadden my heart.

How am I altered by disappointment!—When going to Lisbon, ten years ago, the elasticity of my mind was sufficient to ward off weariness—and the imagination still could dip her brush in the rainbow of fancy, and sketch futurity in smiling colours. Now I am going towards the North in search of sunbeams!—Will any ever warm this desolated heart? All nature seems to frown—or rather mourn with me.—Every thing is cold—cold as my expectations! Before I left the shore, tormented, as I now am, by these North east chillers, I could not help exclaiming—Give me, gracious Heaven! at least, genial weather, if I am never to meet the genial affection that still warms this agitated bosom—compelling life to linger there.

I am now going on shore with the captain, though the weather be rough, to seek for milk, &c. at a little village, and to take a walk—after which I hope to sleep—for, confined here, surrounded by disagreeable smells, I have lost the little appetite I had; and I lie awake, till thinking almost drives me to the brink of madness—only to the brink, for I never forget, even in the feverish slumbers I sometimes fall into, the misery I am labouring to blunt the sense of, by every exertion in my power.

Poor — still continues sick, and — grows weary when the weather will not allow her to remain on deck.

I hope this will be the last letter I shall write from England to you—are you not tired of this lingering adieu?

Yours truly

MARY.

[Hull, June 21, 1795] Sunday Morning.

The captain last night, after I had written my letter to you intended to be left at a little village, offered to go to — to pass to-day. We had a troublesome sail—and now I must hurry on board again, for the wind has changed.

I half expected to find a letter from you here. Had you written one haphazard, it would have been kind and considerate—you might have known, had you thought, that the wind would not permit me to depart. These are attentions, more grateful to the heart than offers of service—But why do I foolishly continue to look for them?

Adieu! adieu! My friend—your friendship is very cold—you see I am hurt.—God bless you! I may perhaps be, some time or other, independent in every sense of the word—Ah! there is but one sense of it of consequence. I will break or bend this weak heart—yet even now it is full.

Yours sincerely
MARY.

The child is well; I did not leave her on board.

[Gothenburg] June 27, Saturday, [1795].

I arrived in Gothenburg this afternoon, after vainly attempting to land at Arendall. I have now but a moment, before the post goes out, to inform you we have got here; though not without considerable difficulty, for we were set ashore in a boat above twenty miles below.

What I suffered in the vessel I will not now descant upon—nor mention the pleasure I received from the sight of the rocky coast.—This morning however, walking to join the carriage that was to transport us to this place, I fell, without any previous warning, senseless on the rocks—and how I escaped with life I can scarcely guess. I was in a stupour for a quarter of an hour; the suffusion of blood at last restored me to my senses—the contusion is great, and my brain confused. The child is well.

Twenty miles ride in the rain, after my accident, has sufficiently deranged me—and here I could not get a fire to warm me, or any thing warm to eat; the inns are mere stables—I must nevertheless go to bed. For God's sake, let me hear from you immediately, my friend! I am not well, and yet you see I cannot die.

Yours sincerely

MARY.

LETTER LIII

[Gothenburg] June 29 [1795].

I wrote to you by the last post, to inform you of my arrival; and I believe I alluded to the extreme fatigue I endured on ship-board, owing to —'s illness, and the roughness of the weather—I likewise mentioned to you my fall, the effects of which I still feel, though I do not think it will have any serious consequences.

— will go with me, if I find it necessary to go to —. The inns here are so bad, I was forced to accept of an apartment in his house. I am overwhelmed with civilities on all sides, and fatigued with the endeavours to amuse me, from which I cannot escape.

My friend—my friend, I am not well—a deadly weight of sorrow lies heavily on my heart. I am again tossed on the troubled billows of life; and obliged to cope with difficulties, without being buoyed up by the hopes that alone render them bearable. "How flat, dull, and unprofitable," appears to me all the bustle into which I see people here so eagerly enter! I long every night to go to bed, to hide my melancholy face in my pillow; but there is a canker-worm in my bosom that never sleeps.

MARY.

LETTER LIV

[Sweden] July 1 [1795].

I labour in vain to calm my mind—my soul has been overwhelmed by sorrow and disappointment. Every thing fatigues me—this is a life that cannot last long. It is you who must determine with respect to futurity—and, when you have, I will act accordingly—I mean, we must either resolve to live together, or part for ever, I cannot bear these continual struggles.—But I wish you to examine carefully your own heart and mind; and, if you perceive the least chance of being happier without me than with me, or if your inclination leans capriciously to that side, do not dissemble; but tell me frankly that you will never see me more. I will then adopt the plan I mentioned to you—for we must either live together, or I will be entirely independent.

My heart is so oppressed, I cannot write with precision—You know however that what I so imperfectly express, are not the crude sentiments of the moment—You can only contribute to my comfort (it is the consolation I am in need of) by being with me—and, if the tenderest friendship is of any value, why will you not look to me for a degree of satisfaction that heartless affections cannot bestow?

Tell me then, will you determine to meet me at Basle?—I shall, I should imagine, be at — before the close of August; and, after you settle your affairs at Paris, could we not meet there?

God bless you!

Yours truly

MARY.

Poor Fanny has suffered during the journey with her teeth.

LETTER LV

[Sweden] July 3 [1795].

There was a gloominess diffused through your last letter, the impression of which still rests on my mind—though, recollecting how quickly you throw off the forcible feelings of the moment, I flatter myself it has long since given place to your usual cheerfulness.

Believe me (and my eyes fill with tears of tenderness as I assure you) there is nothing I would not endure in the way of privation, rather than disturb your tranquillity.—If I am fated to be unhappy, I will labour to hide my sorrows in my own bosom; and you shall always find me a faithful, affectionate friend.

I grow more and more attached to my little girl—and I cherish this affection without fear, because it must be a long time before it can become bitterness of soul.—She is an interesting creature.—On ship-board, how often as I gazed at the sea, have I longed to bury my troubled bosom in the less troubled deep; asserting with Brutus, "that the virtue I had followed too far, was merely an empty name!" and nothing but the sight of her—her playful smiles, which seemed to cling and twine round my heart—could have stopped me.

What peculiar misery has fallen to my share! To act up to my principles, I have laid the strictest restraint on my very thoughts—yes; not to sully the delicacy of my feelings, I have reined in my imagination; and started with affright from every sensation, (I allude to —) that stealing with balmy sweetness into my soul, led me to scent from afar the fragrance of reviving nature.

My friend, I have dearly paid for one conviction.—Love, in some minds, is an affair of sentiment, arising from the same delicacy of perception (or taste) as renders them alive to the beauties of nature, poetry,

&c., alive to the charms of those evanescent graces that are, as it were, impalpable—they must be felt, they cannot be described.

Love is a want of my heart. I have examined myself lately with more care than formerly, and find, that to deaden is not to calm the mind—Aiming at tranquillity, I have almost destroyed all the energy of my soul—almost rooted out what renders it estimable—Yes, I have damped that enthusiasm of character, which converts the grossest materials into a fuel, that imperceptibly feeds hopes, which aspire above common enjoyment. Despair, since the birth of my child, has rendered me stupid—soul and body seemed to be fading away before the withering touch of disappointment.

I am now endeavouring to recover myself—and such is the elasticity of my constitution, and the purity of the atmosphere here, that health unsought for, begins to reanimate my countenance.

I have the sincerest esteem and affection for you—but the desire of regaining peace, (do you understand me?) has made me forget the respect due to my own emotions—sacred emotions, that are the sure harbingers of the delights I was formed to enjoy—and shall enjoy, for nothing can extinguish the heavenly spark.

Still, when we meet again, I will not torment you, I promise you. I blush when I recollect my former conduct—and will not in future confound myself with the beings whom I feel to be my inferiors.—I will listen to delicacy, or pride.

LETTER LVI

[Sweden] July 4 [1795].

I hope to hear from you by to-morrow's mail. My dearest friend! I cannot tear my affections from you— and, though every remembrance stings me to the soul, I think of you, till I make allowance for the very defects of character, that have given such a cruel stab to my peace.

Still however I am more alive, than you have seen me for a long, long time. I have a degree of vivacity, even in my grief, which is preferable to the benumbing stupour that, for the last year, has frozen up all my faculties.—Perhaps this change is more owing to returning health, than to the vigour of my reason— for, in spite of sadness (and surely I have had my share), the purity of this air, and the being continually out in it, for I sleep in the country every night, has made an alteration in my appearance that really surprises me.—The rosy fingers of health already streak my cheeks—and I have seen a physical life in my eyes, after I have been climbing the rocks, that resembled the fond, credulous hopes of youth.

With what a cruel sigh have I recollected that I had forgotten to hope!—Reason, or rather experience, does not thus cruelly damp poor —'s pleasures; she plays all day in the garden with —'s children, and makes friends for herself.

Do not tell me, that you are happier without us—Will you not come to us in Switzerland? Ah, why do not you love us with more sentiment?—why are you a creature of such sympathy, that the warmth of your feelings, or rather quickness of your senses, hardens your heart?—It is my misfortune, that my imagination is perpetually shading your defects, and lending you charms, whilst the grossness of your senses makes you (call me not vain) overlook graces in me, that only dignity of mind, and the sensibility of an expanded heart can give.—God bless you! Adieu.

[Sweden] July 7 [1795].

I could not help feeling extremely mortified last post, at not receiving a letter from you. My being at — was but a chance, and you might have hazarded it; and would a year ago.

I shall not however complain—There are misfortunes so great, as to silence the usual expressions of sorrow—Believe me, there is such a thing as a broken heart! There are characters whose very energy preys upon them; and who, ever inclined to cherish by reflection some passion, cannot rest satisfied with the common comforts of life. I have endeavoured to fly from myself and launched into all the dissipation possible here, only to feel keener anguish, when alone with my child.

Still, could any thing please me—had not disappointment cut me off from life, this romantic country, these fine evenings, would interest me.—My God! can any thing? and am I ever to feel alive only to painful sensations?—But it cannot—it shall not last long.

The post is again arrived; I have sent to seek for letters, only to be wounded to the soul by a negative.—My brain seems on fire. I must go into the air.

MARY.

[Laurvig, Norway] July 14 [1795].

I am now on my journey to Tonsberg. I felt more at leaving my child, than I thought I should—and, whilst at night I imagined every instant that I heard the half-formed sounds of her voice,—I asked myself how I could think of parting with her for ever, of leaving her thus helpless?

Poor lamb! It may run very well in a tale, that "God will temper the winds to the shorn lamb!" but how can I expect that she will be shielded, when my naked bosom has had to brave continually the pitiless storm? Yes; I could add, with poor Lear—What is the war of elements to the pangs of disappointed affection, and the horror arising from a discovery of a breach of confidence, that snaps every social tie!

All is not right somewhere!—When you first knew me, I was not thus lost. I could still confide—for I opened my heart to you—of this only comfort you have deprived me, whilst my happiness, you tell me, was your first object. Strange want of judgment!

I will not complain; but, from the soundness of your understanding, I am convinced, if you give yourself leave to reflect, you will also feel, that your conduct to me, so far from being generous, has not been just.—I mean not to allude to factitious principles of morality; but to the simple basis of all rectitude.—However I did not intend to argue—Your not writing is cruel—and my reason is perhaps disturbed by constant wretchedness.

Poor — would fain have accompanied me, out of tenderness; for my fainting, or rather convulsion, when I landed, and my sudden changes of countenance since, have alarmed her so much, that she is perpetually afraid of some accident.—But it would have injured the child this warm season, as she is cutting her teeth.

I hear not of your having written to me at Stromstad. Very well! Act as you please—there is nothing I fear or care for! When I see whether I can, or cannot obtain the money I am come here about, I will not trouble you with letters to which you do not reply.

LETTER LIX

[Tonsberg] July 18 [1795].

I am here in Tonsberg, separated from my child—and here I must remain a month at least, or I might as well never have come.

I have begun — which will, I hope, discharge all my obligations of a pecuniary kind.—I am lowered in my own eyes, on account of my not having done it sooner.

I shall make no further comments on your silence. God bless you!

MARY.

LETTER LX

[Tonsberg] July 30 [1795].

I have just received two of your letters, dated the 26th and 30th of June; and you must have received several from me, informing you of my detention, and how much I was hurt by your silence.

Write to me then, my friend, and write explicitly. I have suffered, God knows, since I left you. Ah! you have never felt this kind of sickness of heart!—My mind however is at present painfully active, and the sympathy I feel almost rises to agony. But this is not a subject of complaint, it has afforded me pleasure,—and reflected pleasure is all I have to hope for—if a spark of hope be yet alive in my forlorn bosom.

I will try to write with a degree of composure. I wish for us to live together, because I want you to acquire an habitual tenderness for my poor girl. I cannot bear to think of leaving her alone in the world, or that she should only be protected by your sense of duty. Next to preserving her, my most earnest wish is not to disturb your peace. I have nothing to expect, and little to fear, in life—There are wounds that can never be healed—but they may be allowed to fester in silence without wincing.

When we meet again, you shall be convinced that I have more resolution than you give me credit for. I will not torment you. If I am destined always to be disappointed and unhappy, I will conceal the anguish I cannot dissipate; and the tightened cord of life or reason will at last snap, and set me free.

Yes; I shall be happy—This heart is worthy of the bliss its feelings anticipate—and I cannot even persuade myself, wretched as they have made me, that my principles and sentiments are not founded in nature and truth. But to have done with these subjects.

I have been seriously employed in this way since I came to Tonsberg; yet I never was so much in the air.—I walk, I ride on horseback—row, bathe, and even sleep in the fields; my health is consequently improved. The child, — informs me, is well, I long to be with her.

Write to me immediately—were I only to think of myself, I could wish you to return to me, poor, with the simplicity of character, part of which you seem lately to have lost, that first attached to you.

Yours most affectionately   MARY IMLAY

I have been subscribing other letters—so I mechanically did the same to yours.

LETTER LXI

[Tonsberg] August 5 [1795].

Employment and exercise have been of great service to me; and I have entirely recovered the strength and activity I lost during the time of my nursing. I have seldom been in better health; and my mind, though trembling to the touch of anguish, is calmer—yet still the same.—I have, it is true, enjoyed some tranquillity, and more happiness here, than for a long—long time past.—(I say happiness, for I can give no other appellation to the exquisite delight this wild country and fine summer have afforded me.)— Still, on examining my heart, I find that it is so constituted, I cannot live without some particular affection—I am afraid not without a passion—and I feel the want of it more in society, than in solitude.

Writing to you, whenever an affectionate epithet occurs—my eyes fill with tears, and my trembling hand stops—you may then depend on my resolution, when with you. If I am doomed to be unhappy, I will confine my anguish in my own bosom—tenderness, rather than passion, has made me sometimes overlook delicacy—the same tenderness will in future restrain me. God bless you!

LETTER LXII

[Tonsberg] August 7 [1795].

Air, exercise, and bathing, have restored me to health, braced my muscles, and covered my ribs, even whilst I have recovered my former activity.—I cannot tell you that my mind is calm, though I have snatched some moments of exquisite delight, wandering through the woods, and resting on the rocks.

This state of suspense, my friend, is intolerable; we must determine on something—and soon;—we must meet shortly, or part for ever. I am sensible that I acted foolishly—but I was wretched—when we were together—Expecting too much, I let the pleasure I might have caught, slip from me. I cannot live with you—I ought not—if you form another attachment. But I promise you, mine shall not be intruded on you. Little reason have I to expect a shadow of happiness, after the cruel disappointments that have rent my heart; but that of my child seems to depend on our being together. Still I do not wish you to sacrifice a chance of enjoyment for an uncertain good. I feel a conviction, that I can provide for her, and it shall be my object—if we are indeed to part to meet no more. Her affection must not be divided. She must be a comfort to me—if I am to have no other—and only know me as her support. I feel that I cannot endure the anguish of corresponding with you—if we are only to correspond.—No; if you seek for happiness elsewhere, my letters shall not interrupt your repose. I will be dead to you. I cannot express to you what pain it gives me to write about an eternal separation.—You must determine— examine yourself—But, for God's sake! spare me the anxiety of uncertainty!—I may sink under the trial; but I will not complain.

Adieu! If I had any thing more to say to you, it is all flown, and absorbed by the most tormenting apprehensions; yet I scarcely know what new form of misery I have to dread.

I ought to beg your pardon for having sometimes written peevishly; but you will impute it to affection, if you understand anything of the heart of

Yours truly

MARY.

LETTER LXIII

[Tonsberg] August 9 [1795].

Five of your letters have been sent after me from —. One, dated the 14th of July, was written in a style which I may have merited, but did not expect from you. However this is not a time to reply to it, except to assure you that you shall not be tormented with any more complaints. I am disgusted with myself for having so long importuned you with my affection.—

My child is very well. We shall soon meet, to part no more, I hope—I mean, I and my girl.—I shall wait with some degree of anxiety till I am informed how your affairs terminate.

Yours sincerely

MARY.

[Gothenburg] August 26 [1795].

I arrived here last night, and with the most exquisite delight, once more pressed my babe to my heart. We shall part no more. You perhaps cannot conceive the pleasure it gave me, to see her run about, and play alone. Her increasing intelligence attaches me more and more to her. I have promised her that I will fulfil my duty to her; and nothing in future shall make me forget it. I will also exert myself to obtain an independence for her; but I will not be too anxious on this head.

I have already told you, that I have recovered my health. Vigour, and even vivacity of mind, have returned with a renovated constitution. As for peace, we will not talk of it. I was not made, perhaps, to enjoy the calm contentment so termed.—

You tell me that my letters torture you; I will not describe the effect yours have on me. I received three this morning, the last dated the 7th of this month. I mean not to give vent to the emotions they produced.—Certainly you are right; our minds are not congenial. I have lived in an ideal world, and fostered sentiments that you do not comprehend—or you would not treat me thus. I am not, I will not be, merely an object of compassion—a clog, however light, to teize you. Forget that I exist: I will never remind you. Something emphatical whispers me to put an end to these struggles. Be free—I will not torment, when I cannot please. I can take care of my child; you need not continually tell me that our fortune is inseparable, that you will try to cherish tenderness for me. Do no violence to yourself! When we are separated, our interest, since you give so much weight to pecuniary considerations, will be entirely divided. I want not protection without affection; and support I need not, whilst my faculties are undisturbed. I had a dislike to living in England; but painful feelings must give way to superior considerations. I may not be able to acquire the sum necessary to maintain my child and self elsewhere. It is too late to go to Switzerland. I shall not remain at —, living expensively. But be not alarmed! I shall not force myself on you any more.

Adieu! I am agitated—my whole frame is convulsed—my lips tremble, as if shook by cold, though fire seems to be circulating in my veins.

God bless you.

MARY.

[Copenhagen] September 6 [1795].

I received just now your letter of the 20th. I had written you a letter last night, into which imperceptibly slipt some of my bitterness of soul. I will copy the part relative to business. I am not sufficiently vain to imagine that I can, for more than a moment, cloud your enjoyment of life—to prevent even that, you had better never hear from me—and repose on the idea that I am happy.

Gracious God! It is impossible for me to stifle something like resentment, when I receive fresh proofs of your indifference. What I have suffered this last year, is not to be forgotten! I have not that happy substitute for wisdom, insensibility—and the lively sympathies which bind me to my fellow-creatures, are all of a painful kind.—They are the agonies of a broken heart—pleasure and I have shaken hands.

I see here nothing but heaps of ruins, and only converse with people immersed in trade and sensuality.

I am weary of travelling—yet seem to have no home—no resting-place to look to.—I am strangely cast off.—How often, passing through the rocks, I have thought, "But for this child, I would lay my head on one of them, and never open my eyes again!" With a heart feelingly alive to all the affections of my nature—I have never met with one, softer than the stone that I would fain take for my last pillow. I once thought I had, but it was all a delusion. I meet with families continually, who are bound together by affection or principle—and, when I am conscious that I have fulfilled the duties of my station, almost to a forgetfulness of myself, I am ready to demand, in a murmuring tone, of Heaven, "Why am I thus abandoned?"

You say now

I do not understand you. It is necessary for you to write more explicitly—and determine on some mode of conduct.—I cannot endure this suspense—Decide—Do you fear to strike another blow? We live together, or eternally part!—I shall not write to you again, till I receive an answer to this. I must compose my tortured soul, before I write on indifferent subjects.

I do not know whether I write intelligibly, for my head is disturbed. But this you ought to pardon—for it is with difficulty frequently that I make out what you mean to say—You write, I suppose, at Mr. —'s after dinner, when your head is not the clearest—and as for your heart, if you have one, I see nothing like the dictates of affection, unless a glimpse when you mention the child—Adieu!

LETTER LXVI

[Hamburg] September 25 [1795].

I have just finished a letter, to be given in charge to captain —. In that I complained of your silence, and expressed my surprise that three mails should have arrived without bringing a line for me. Since I closed it, I hear of another, and still no letter.—I am labouring to write calmly—this silence is a refinement on cruelty. Had captain — remained a few days longer, I would have returned with him to England. What have I to do here? I have repeatedly written to you fully. Do you do the same—and quickly. Do not leave me in suspense. I have not deserved this of you. I cannot write, my mind is so distressed. Adieu!

MARY.

LETTER LXVII

[Hamburg] September 27 [1795].

When you receive this, I shall either have landed, or be hovering on the British coast—your letter of the 18th decided me.

By what criterion of principle or affection, you term my questions extraordinary and unnecessary, I cannot determine.—You desire me to decide—I had decided. You must have had long ago two letters of mine, from —, to the same purport, to consider.—In these, God knows! there was but too much affection, and the agonies of a distracted mind were but too faithfully pourtrayed!—What more then had I to say?—The negative was to come from you.—You had perpetually recurred to your promise of meeting me in the autumn—Was it extraordinary that I should demand a yes, or no?—Your letter is written with extreme harshness, coldness I am accustomed to, in it I find not a trace of the tenderness of humanity, much less of friendship.—I only see a desire to heave a load off your shoulders.

I am above disputing about words.—It matters not in what terms you decide.

The tremendous power who formed this heart, must have foreseen that, in a world in which self-interest, in various shapes, is the principal mobile, I had little chance of escaping misery.—To the fiat of fate I submit.—I am content to be wretched; but I will not be contemptible.—Of me you have no cause to complain, but for having had too much regard for you—for having expected a degree of permanent happiness, when you only sought for a momentary gratification.

I am strangely deficient in sagacity.—Uniting myself to you, your tenderness seemed to make me amends for all my former misfortunes.—On this tenderness and affection with what confidence did I rest!—but I leaned on a spear, that has pierced me to the heart.—You have thrown off a faithful friend, to pursue the caprices of the moment.—We certainly are differently organized; for even now, when conviction has been stamped on my soul by sorrow, I can scarcely believe it possible. It depends at present on you, whether you will see me or not.—I shall take no step, till I see or hear from you.

Preparing myself for the worst—I have determined, if your next letter be like the last, to write to Mr. — to procure me an obscure lodging, and not to inform any body of my arrival.—There I will endeavour in a few months to obtain the sum necessary to take me to France—from you I will not receive any more.—I am not yet sufficiently humbled to depend on your beneficence.

Some people, whom my unhappiness has interested, though they know not the extent of it, will assist me to attain the object I have in view, the independence of my child. Should a peace take place, ready money will go a great way in France—and I will borrow a sum, which my industry shall enable me to pay at my leisure, to purchase a small estate for my girl.—The assistance I shall find necessary to complete her education, I can get at an easy rate at Paris—I can introduce her to such society as she will like—and thus, securing for her all the chance for happiness, which depends on me, I shall die in peace, persuaded that the felicity which has hitherto cheated my expectation, will not always elude my grasp. No poor temptest-tossed mariner ever more earnestly longed to arrive at his port.

MARY.

I shall not come up in the vessel all the way, because I have no place to go to. Captain — will inform you where I am. It is needless to add, that I am not in a state of mind to bear suspense—and that I wish to see you, though it be for the last time.

[Dover] Sunday, October 4 [1795].

I wrote to you by the packet, to inform you, that your letter of the 18th of last month, had determined me to set out with captain —; but, as we sailed very quick, I take it for granted, that you have not yet received it.

You say, I must decide for myself.—I had decided, that it was most for the interest of my little girl, and for my own comfort, little as I expect, for us to live together; and I even thought that you would be glad, some years hence, when the tumult of business was over, to repose in the society of an affectionate friend, and mark the progress of our interesting child, whilst endeavouring to be of use in the circle you at last resolved to rest in: for you cannot run about for ever.

From the tenour of your last letter however, I am led to imagine, that you have formed some new attachment.—If it be so, let me earnestly request you to see me once more, and immediately. This is the only proof I require of the friendship you profess for me. I will then decide, since you boggle about a mere form.

I am labouring to write with calmness—but the extreme anguish I feel, at landing without having any friend to receive me, and even to be conscious that the friend whom I most wish to see, will feel a disagreeable sensation at being informed of my arrival, does not come under the description of common misery. Every emotion yields to an overwhelming flood of sorrow—and the playfulness of my child distresses me.—On her account, I wished to remain a few days here, comfortless as is my situation.— Besides, I did not wish to surprise you. You have told me, that you would make any sacrifice to promote my happiness—and, even in your last unkind letter, you talk of the ties which bind you to me and my child.—Tell me, that you wish it, and I will cut this Gordian knot.

I now most earnestly intreat you to write to me, without fail, by the return of the post. Direct your letter to be left at the post-office, and tell me whether you will come to me here, or where you will meet me. I can receive your letter on Wednesday morning.

Do not keep me in suspense.—I expect nothing from you, or any human being: my die is cast!—I have fortitude enough to determine to do my duty; yet I cannot raise my depressed spirits, or calm my trembling heart.—That being who moulded it thus, knows that I am unable to tear up by the roots the propensity to affection which has been the torment of my life—but life will have an end!

Should you come here (a few months ago I could not have doubted it) you will find me at —. If you prefer meeting me on the road, tell me where.

Yours affectionately,   MARY.

[London, Nov. 1795].

I write to you now on my knees; imploring you to send my child and the maid with —, to Paris, to be consigned to the care of Madame —, rue —, section de —. Should they be removed, — can give their direction.

Let the maid have all my clothes, without distinction.

Pray pay the cook her wages, and do not mention the confession which I forced from her—a little sooner or later is of no consequence. Nothing but my extreme stupidity could have rendered me blind so long. Yet, whilst you assured me that you had no attachment, I thought we might still have lived together.

I shall make no comments on your conduct; or any appeal to the world. Let my wrongs sleep with me! Soon, very soon shall I be at peace. When you receive this, my burning head will be cold.

I would encounter a thousand deaths, rather than a night like the last. Your treatment has thrown my mind into a state of chaos; yet I am serene. I go to find comfort, and my only fear is, that my poor body will be insulted by an endeavour to recal my hated existence. But I shall plunge into the Thames where there is the least chance of my being snatched from the death I seek.

God bless you! May you never know by experience what you have made me endure. Should your sensibility ever awake, remorse will find its way to your heart; and, in the midst of business and sensual pleasure, I shall appear before you, the victim of your deviation from rectitude.

MARY.

LETTER LXX

[London, Nov. 1795] Sunday Morning.

I have only to lament, that, when the bitterness of death was past, I was inhumanly brought back to life and misery. But a fixed determination is not to be baffled by disappointment; nor will I allow that to be a frantic attempt, which was one of the calmest acts of reason. In this respect, I am only accountable to myself. Did I care for what is termed reputation, it is by other circumstances that I should be dishonoured.

You say, "that you know not how to extricate ourselves out of the wretchedness into which we have been plunged." You are extricated long since.—But I forbear to comment.—If I am condemned to live longer, it is a living death.

It appears to me, that you lay much more stress on delicacy, than on principle; for I am unable to discover what sentiment of delicacy would have been violated, by your visiting a wretched friend—if indeed you have any friendship for me.—But since your new attachment is the only thing sacred in your eyes, I am silent—Be happy! My complaints shall never more damp your enjoyment—perhaps I am mistaken in supposing that even my death could, for more than a moment.—This is what you call magnanimity.—It is happy for yourself, that you possess this quality in the highest degree.

Your continually asserting, that you will do all in your power to contribute to my comfort (when you only allude to pecuniary assistance), appears to me a flagrant breach of delicacy.—I want not such vulgar comfort, nor will I accept it. I never wanted but your heart—That gone, you have nothing more to give. Had I only poverty to fear, I should not shrink from life.—Forgive me then, if I say, that I shall consider any direct or indirect attempt to supply my necessities, as an insult which I have not merited—and as rather done out of tenderness for your own reputation, than for me. Do not mistake me; I do not think that you value money (therefore I will not accept what you do not care for) though I do much less, because certain privations are not painful to me. When I am dead, respect for yourself will make you take care of the child.

I write with difficulty—probably I shall never write to you again.—Adieu!

God bless you!

MARY.

LETTER LXXI

[London, Nov. 1795] Monday Morning.

I am compelled at last to say that you treat me ungenerously. I agree with you, that

But let the obliquity now fall on me.—I fear neither poverty nor infamy. I am unequal to the task of writing—and explanations are not necessary.

My child may have to blush for her mother's want of prudence—and may lament that the rectitude of my heart made me above vulgar precautions; but she shall not despise me for meanness.—You are now perfectly free.—God bless you.

MARY.

LETTER LXXII

[London, Nov. 1795] Saturday Night.

I have been hurt by indirect enquiries, which appear to me not to be dictated by any tenderness to me.—You ask "If I am well or tranquil?"—They who think me so, must want a heart to estimate my feelings by.—I chuse then to be the organ of my own sentiments.

I must tell you, that I am very much mortified by your continually offering me pecuniary assistance— and, considering your going to the new house, as an open avowal that you abandon me, let me tell you that I will sooner perish than receive any thing from you—and I say this at the moment when I am disappointed in my first attempt to obtain a temporary supply. But this even pleases me; an accumulation of disappointments and misfortunes seems to suit the habit of my mind.—

Have but a little patience, and I will remove myself where it will not be necessary for you to talk—of course, not to think of me. But let me see, written by yourself—for I will not receive it through any other medium—that the affair is finished.—It is an insult to me to suppose, that I can be reconciled, or recover my spirits; but, if you hear nothing of me, it will be the same thing to you.

MARY.

Even your seeing me, has been to oblige other people, and not to sooth my distracted mind.

[London, Nov. 1795] Thursday Afternoon.

Mr. — having forgot to desire you to send the things of mine which were left at the house, I have to request you to let — bring them to —

I shall go this evening to the lodging; so you need not be restrained from coming here to transact your business.—And, whatever I may think, and feel—you need not fear that I shall publicly complain—No! If I have any criterion to judge of right and wrong, I have been most ungenerously treated: but, wishing now only to hide myself, I shall be silent as the grave in which I long to forget myself. I shall protect and provide for my child.—I only mean by this to say, that you have nothing to fear from my desperation.

Farewell.

MARY.

London, November 27 [1795].

The letter, without an address, which you put up with the letters you returned, did not meet my eyes till just now.—I had thrown the letters aside—I did not wish to look over a register of sorrow.

My not having seen it, will account for my having written to you with anger—under the impression your departure, without even a line left for me, made on me, even after your late conduct, which could not lead me to expect much attention to my sufferings.

In fact, "the decided conduct, which appeared to me so unfeeling," has almost overturned my reason; my mind is injured—I scarcely know where I am, or what I do.—The grief I cannot conquer (for some cruel recollections never quit me, banishing almost every other) I labour to conceal in total solitude.—

My life therefore is but an exercise of fortitude, continually on the stretch—and hope never gleams in this tomb, where I am buried alive.

But I meant to reason with you, and not to complain.—You tell me, that I shall judge more coolly of your mode of acting, some time hence." But is it not possible that passion clouds your reason, as much as it does mine?—and ought you not to doubt, whether those principles are so "exalted," as you term them, which only lead to your own gratification? In other words, whether it be just to have no principle of action, but that of following your inclination, trampling on the affection you have fostered, and the expectations you have excited?

My affection for you is rooted in my heart.—I know you are not what you now seem—nor will you always act, or feel, as you now do, though I may never be comforted by the change.—Even at Paris, my image will haunt you.—You will see my pale face—and sometimes the tears of anguish will drop on your heart; which you have forced from mine.

I cannot write. I thought I could quickly have refuted all your ingenious arguments; but my head is confused.—Right or wrong, I am miserable!

It seems to me, that my conduct has always been governed by the strictest principles of justice and truth.—Yet, how wretched have my social feelings, and delicacy of sentiment rendered me!—I have loved with my whole soul, only to discover that I had no chance of a return—and that existence is a burthen without it.

I do not perfectly understand you.—If, by the offer of your friendship, you still only mean pecuniary support—I must again reject it.—Trifling are the ills of poverty in the scale of my misfortunes.—God bless you!

MARY.

I have been treated ungenerously—if I understand what is generosity.—You seem to me only to have been anxious to shake me off—regardless whether you dashed me to atoms by the fall.—In truth I have been rudely handled. Do you judge coolly, and I trust you will not continue to call those capricious feelings "the most refined," which would undermine not only the most sacred principles, but the affections which unite mankind.—You would render mothers unnatural—and there would be no such thing as a father!—If your theory of morals is the most "exalted," it is certainly the most easy.—It does not require much magnanimity, to determine to please ourselves for the moment, let others suffer what they will!

Excuse me for again tormenting you, my heart thirsts for justice from you—and whilst I recollect that you approved Miss —'s conduct—I am convinced you will not always justify your own.

Beware of the deceptions of passion! It will not always banish from your mind, that you have acted ignobly—and condescended to subterfuge to gloss over the conduct you could not excuse.—Do truth and principle require such sacrifices?

LETTER LXXV

London, December 8 [1795].

Having just been informed that — is to return immediately to Paris, I would not miss a sure opportunity of writing, because I am not certain that my last, by Dover has reached you.

Resentment, and even anger, are momentary emotions with me—and I wished to tell you so, that if you ever think of me, it may not be in the light of an enemy.

That I have not been used well I must ever feel; perhaps, not always with the keen anguish I do at present—for I began even now to write calmly, and I cannot restrain my tears.

I am stunned!—Your late conduct still appears to me a frightful dream.—Ah! ask yourself if you have not condescended to employ a little address, I could almost say cunning, unworthy of you?—Principles are sacred things—and we never play with truth, with impunity.

The expectation (I have too fondly nourished it) of regaining your affection, every day grows fainter and fainter.—Indeed, it seems to me, when I am more sad than usual, that I shall never see you more.—Yet you will not always forget me.—You will feel something like remorse, for having lived only for yourself— and sacrificed my peace to inferior gratifications. In a comfortless old age, you will remember that you had one disinterested friend, whose heart you wounded to the quick. The hour of recollection will come—and you will not be satisfied to act the part of a boy, till you fall into that of a dotard. I know that your mind, your heart, and your principles of action, are all superior to your present conduct. You do, you must, respect me—and you will be sorry to forfeit my esteem.

You know best whether I am still preserving the remembrance of an imaginary being.—I once thought that I knew you thoroughly—but now I am obliged to leave some doubts that involuntarily press on me, to be cleared up by time.

You may render me unhappy; but cannot make me contemptible in my own eyes.—I shall still be able to support my child, though I am disappointed in some other plans of usefulness, which I once believed would have afforded you equal pleasure.

Whilst I was with you, I restrained my natural generosity, because I thought your property in jeopardy.— When I went to [Sweden], I requested you, if you could conveniently, not to forget my father, sisters, and some other people, whom I was interested about.—Money was lavished away, yet not only my requests were neglected, but some trifling debts were not discharged, that now come on me.—Was this friendship—or generosity? Will you not grant you have forgotten yourself? Still I have an affection for you.—God bless you.

MARY.

LETTER LXXVI

[London, Dec. 1795.]

As the parting from you for ever is the most serious event of my life, I will once expostulate with you, and call not the language of truth and feeling ingenuity!

I know the soundness of your understanding—and know that it is impossible for you always to confound the caprices of every wayward inclination with the manly dictates of principle.

You tell me "that I torment you."—Why do I?—Because you cannot estrange your heart entirely from me—and you feel that justice is on my side. You urge, "that your conduct was unequivocal."—It was not.—When your coolness has hurt me, with what tenderness have you endeavoured to remove the impression!—and even before I returned to England, you took great pains to convince me, that all my uneasiness was occasioned by the effect of a worn-out constitution—and you concluded your letter with these words, "Business alone has kept me from you.—Come to any port, and I will fly down to my two dear girls with a heart all their own."

With these assurances, is it extraordinary that I should believe what I wished? I might—and did think that you had a struggle with old propensities; but I still thought that I and virtue should at last prevail. I still thought that you had a magnanimity of character, which would enable you to conquer yourself.

Imlay, believe me, it is not romance, you have acknowledged to me feelings of this kind.—You could restore me to life and hope, and the satisfaction you would feel, would amply repay you.

In tearing myself from you, it is my own heart I pierce—and the time will come, when you will lament that you have thrown away a heart, that, even in the moment of passion, you cannot despise.—I would owe every thing to your generosity—but, for God's sake, keep me no longer in suspense!—Let me see you once more!—

LETTER LXXVII

[London, Dec. 1795.]

You must do as you please with respect to the child.—I could wish that it might be done soon, that my name may be no more mentioned to you. It is now finished.—Convinced that you have neither regard nor friendship, I disdain to utter a reproach, though I have had reason to think, that the "forbearance" talked of, has not been very delicate.—It is however of no consequence.—I am glad you are satisfied with your own conduct.

I now solemnly assure you, that this is an eternal farewel.—Yet I flinch not from the duties which tie me to life.

That there is "sophistry" on one side or other, is certain; but now it matters not on which. On my part it has not been a question of words. Yet your understanding or mine must be strangely warped—for what you term "delicacy," appears to me to be exactly the contrary. I have no criterion for morality, and have thought in vain, if the sensations which lead you to follow an ancle or step, be the sacred foundation of principle and affection. Mine has been of a very different nature, or it would not have stood the brunt of your sarcasms.

The sentiment in me is still sacred. If there be any part of me that will survive the sense of my misfortunes, it is the purity of my affections. The impetuosity of your senses, may have led you to term mere animal desire, the source of principle; and it may give zest to some years to come.—Whether you will always think so, I shall never know.

It is strange that, in spite of all you do, something like conviction forces me to believe, that you are not what you appear to be.

I part with you in peace.

FOOTNOTES

[1] Dowden's "Life of Shelley."

[2] The child is in a subsequent letter called the "barrier girl," probably from a supposition that she owed her existence to this interview.—W. G.

[3] This and the thirteen following letters appear to have been written during a separation of several months; the date, Paris.—W. G.

[4] Some further letters, written during the remainder of the week, in a similar strain to the preceding, appear to have been destroyed by the person to whom they were addressed.—W. G.

[5] Imlay went to Paris on March 11, after spending a fortnight at Havre, but he returned to Mary soon after the date of Letter XIX. In August he went to Paris, where he was followed by Mary. In September Imlay visited London on business.

[6] The child spoken of in some preceding letters, had now been born a considerable time. She was born, May 14, 1794, and was named Fanny.—W. G.

[7] She means, "the latter more than the former."—W. G.

[8] This is the first of a series of letters written during a separation of many months, to which no cordial meeting ever succeeded. They were sent from Paris, and bear the address of London.—W. G.

[9] The person to whom the letters are addressed [Imlay], was about this time at Ramsgate, on his return, as he professed, to Paris, when he was recalled, as it should seem, to London, by the further pressure of business now accumulated upon him.—W. G.

[10] This probably alludes to some expression of [Imlay] the person to whom the letters are addressed, in which he treated as common evils, things upon which the letter-writer was disposed to bestow a different appellation.—W. G.

[11] This passage refers to letters written under a purpose of suicide, and not intended to be opened till after the catastrophe.—W. G.

www.ingramcontent.com/pod-product-compliance
Lightning Source LLC
Chambersburg PA
CBHW021938170626
46807CB00007B/3170